Their gazes connected.

Joelle had to be experiencing a whirl of emotions right now. He certainly was. Duncan lowered his head and touched his mouth to hers. Just a touch, but it packed a punch.

Man, did it.

The heat would have rolled right through him, and he wanted to take her mouth as he'd done the night they'd landed in bed. And they would have both paid dearly for that lapse, too. He and Joelle already had enough regrets, and Duncan didn't want this to be one of them. He figured Joelle felt the same.

He was wrong.

Joelle came up on her toes and kissed him. Not a touch this time. It was hard, hungry and filled with emotions. So much heat. She seemed to be using it as an anchor, too. Or maybe something that would help her remember that she was alive.

"Thank you," she said when she finally pulled back. "You saved my life. You saved the baby."

THE SHERIFF'S BABY

USA TODAY BESTSELLING AUTHOR
DELORES FOSSEN

INTRIGUE

Harlequin® INTRIGUE™

Recycling programs for this product may not exist in your area.

ISBN-13: 978-1-335-45696-0

The Sheriff's Baby

Copyright © 2024 by Delores Fossen

All rights reserved. No part of this book may be used or reproduced in any manner whatsoever without written permission.

Without limiting the author's and publisher's exclusive rights, any unauthorized use of this publication to train generative artificial intelligence (AI) technologies is expressly prohibited.

This is a work of fiction. Names, characters, places and incidents are either the product of the author's imagination or are used fictitiously. Any resemblance to actual persons, living or dead, businesses, companies, events or locales is entirely coincidental.

For questions and comments about the quality of this book, please contact us at CustomerService@Harlequin.com.

TM and ® are trademarks of Harlequin Enterprises ULC.

Harlequin Enterprises ULC
22 Adelaide St. West, 41st Floor
Toronto, Ontario M5H 4E3, Canada
www.Harlequin.com

Printed in Lithuania

MIX
Paper | Supporting responsible forestry
FSC® C021394

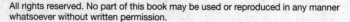

Delores Fossen, a *USA TODAY* bestselling author, has written over 150 novels, with millions of copies of her books in print worldwide. She's received a Booksellers' Best Award and an RT Reviewers' Choice Best Book Award. She was also a finalist for a prestigious RITA® Award. You can contact the author through her website at deloresfossen.com.

Books by Delores Fossen

Harlequin Intrigue

Saddle Ridge Justice

The Sheriff's Baby

Silver Creek Lawman: Second Generation

Targeted in Silver Creek
Maverick Detective Dad
Last Seen in Silver Creek
Marked for Revenge

The Law in Lubbock County

Sheriff in the Saddle
Maverick Justice
Lawman to the Core
Spurred to Justice

Mercy Ridge Lawmen

Her Child to Protect
Safeguarding the Surrogate
Targeting the Deputy
Pursued by the Sheriff

Visit the Author Profile page at Harlequin.com.

CAST OF CHARACTERS

Sheriff Duncan Holder—Sheriff of Saddle Ridge, Texas. He'll do whatever it takes to protect his ex, Deputy Joelle McCullough, and their unborn child.

Deputy Joelle McCullough—She's five months pregnant, and even though things are strained between Duncan and her, she'll work with him to stop the threat to their baby.

Molly Radel—A dispatcher who's kidnapped the same night someone attempts to abduct Joelle. It's possible these attacks are linked to the murder of Joelle's father, which happened five years ago.

Al Hamlin—A PI who claims he's looking for his missing pregnant sister, but it's possible he's the one behind the attacks.

Brad Moreland—He has an axe to grind with everyone in Saddle Ridge for what he feels is a wrongful arrest of his now ex-wife.

Shanda Cantrell—Brad's ex-wife. She miscarried after being arrested by Joelle's father, who was then sheriff. She insists she's gotten over the past but could be planning revenge.

Kate Moreland—Brad's mother. She's been linked to the illegal sale of babies, so she might have her own agenda for wanting to kidnap Joelle.

Chapter One

The sound instantly woke Deputy Joelle McCullough, but it took her a moment to realize it hadn't been part of the dream.

The nightmare.

There were no blasts of gunshots that had killed her father. No, this had been a clicking sound like that of someone shutting a vehicle door.

Rubbing her eyes to help her focus, Joelle checked her phone for the time. Just past 2:00 a.m., which meant it wasn't anywhere near a normal visiting hour. Added to that, she wasn't exactly on the beaten path since her house was a good mile outside of her hometown of Saddle Ridge with no other houses within sight of hers.

There were no texts from her three siblings or any of her friends. None either from anyone at the Saddle Ridge Sheriff's Office where she'd been a deputy for seven years now. So, no alerts from anyone she knew well enough to contact her before just showing up at her place, but it could be a neighbor coming to her for help.

Everyone in Saddle Ridge knew where she lived, knew that she was a cop. That meant this could be some kind of emergency that had warranted a face-to-face rather than a call or text.

She threw back the covers, immediately reaching for her

Glock 22 that she kept on the nightstand. Grabbing her firearm when off duty hadn't always been her automatic response. Not until five months ago when her father had been gunned down at his home. Since then, things had changed.

Everything had changed.

And Joelle no longer trusted that a neighbor's emergency—or whatever this was—wouldn't end in gunfire. Her father hadn't been armed when he'd answered his door that night. He obviously hadn't been alarmed that whoever had come calling was there to kill him.

She couldn't make the same mistake.

It was the reason she'd had a top-notch security system installed, and it was turned on and armed. If anyone attempted to get in through a door or window, the alarms would start blaring, and the security company and the sheriff's office would be alerted. Most importantly, *she* would be alerted, and she could use her cop's training to put a stop to a threat.

Despite the urgency and worry building inside her, Joelle took her time getting out of bed. She'd learned the hard way that standing too quickly would make her lightheaded.

One of the side effects of being five months pregnant.

She ran her hand over her stomach, trying to soothe the baby's sudden fluttering. Not hard kicks. Not yet, anyway. Just soft stirrings that reminded her of the precious cargo she was carrying. Reminding her again of why she couldn't risk what'd happened to her father.

Once her heartbeat had steadied enough so that it was no longer thrumming in her ears, Joelle listened for any other sounds. Nothing except for the hum of the air conditioner and the spring breeze rattling through some of the tree branches outside her house.

She went to the front window and peered out, but it

took her a moment to spot the vehicle. A black car that she didn't recognize. It was parked not in her driveway but off to the side beneath a pair of towering oaks. The headlights weren't on, and the door was indeed shut.

There was no sign of the driver.

Because of the angle of the parked car, Joelle couldn't see the license plates, and she didn't waste time figuring out what was going on. Not with every one of her cop's instincts now telling her that something was wrong. She stepped to the side of the window so that she wouldn't be seen or in the line of fire, and made a call to the Saddle Ridge dispatcher.

"This is Deputy Joelle McCullough," she said, keeping her voice at a whisper just in case the driver of that vehicle was close enough to hear her. "I need backup at my house."

She wasn't sure who was on night duty at the sheriff's office, but it wouldn't be her brother Slater. He was staying the night in San Antonio, a thirty-minute drive away, since he was on the schedule to testify at a trial. If Slater had been in town, she would have called him directly since he lived just up the road from her.

After she'd done a thorough visual sweep of the front exterior of her house, Joelle went to her kitchen window to check the backyard. Thankfully, there was a full moon to give her some visibility, but there were also plenty of trees and shrubs dotting the five acres she owned. Lots of places for someone to hide if that's what a person wanted to do to try to get back at a cop.

She wasn't aware of anyone specifically who wanted to end her life or get revenge on her, but her father's killer was still unknown and at large. Since no one was certain of the reason her dad had been gunned down, she might be on the killer's hit list, too.

With her phone in her left hand and the Glock still gripped in her right, Joelle stayed positioned to the side of the kitchen window while she continued to watch and listen. Nothing.

And that in itself was troubling.

If this was someone she knew, they would have already come to the door or made themselves known. Added to that, the person would have parked in front of her house and not off to the side like that.

The minutes crawled by until Joelle saw the slash of headlights as they turned into her driveway. Backup, no doubt. She didn't breathe easier, though, because she needed to let the responding deputy know there was someone out there, maybe someone waiting to fire shots.

She hurried back to the front and silently cursed when she glanced out the front window and recognized the dark blue truck. Not a deputy but rather Sheriff Duncan Holder. Once, he'd been a fellow deputy but had been elected sheriff after her father's death.

Duncan was also the father of her unborn child.

As always, she got a serious jolt of conflicted feelings whenever she laid eyes on Duncan. Memories. Heat. Guilt. Grief. A bundle of raw nerves mixed with the old attraction that Joelle wished wasn't there.

Because she didn't want Duncan or anyone else to be gunned down tonight, Joelle fired off a quick text to let him know about the unfamiliar black car and the out-of-sight driver. Duncan responded just seconds later with a thumbs-up emoji, and he pulled his truck into her yard and closer to her porch. He sat there for a few moments, still on his phone, and Joelle figured he was probably running the license plate on the visitor's vehicle since he'd likely have a good view of the one on the rear of the car.

Duncan finally put his phone away and stepped from his truck, keeping cover behind the door while he fired glances around the yard. He, too, had his Glock drawn and ready.

Her heart did that stupid little flutter it always did whenever she was around him, and for the umpteenth time, Joelle wished she could make herself immune to him. Hard to do, though, with those unforgettable, heart-fluttering looks. The dark brown hair, blue eyes and a face that had no doubt gotten him plenty of lustful looks.

More seconds passed. Her heart raced. Adrenaline pumped through her. Her stomach tightened.

The gusts of wind sure didn't help, either, with her raw, edgy nerves. Those gusts kicked up, stirring seemingly everything at once, including an owl that sounded agitated by the noise. It was bad timing since the owl's hoots and squawks could conceal any sounds her visitor might make.

Duncan finally moved away from his truck, coming up the porch steps, and that was her cue to use her phone app to disarm the security system and unlock the door. He stepped in and brought the scent of the fresh night air with him. His own scent, too, one she wished wasn't so familiar to her.

"You're not on shift," she muttered, well aware that her tone wasn't exactly friendly.

"No. I couldn't sleep so I went into the office to do some paperwork. I was there when you called. Have you seen anyone around that car or the house?" he tacked onto that.

He met her gaze for just a fraction. She was betting that he was also trying to make himself immune to her.

Joelle shook her head, locked the door and reset the security system. "I heard the car door shut about fifteen minutes ago. It woke me, and when I got up and didn't see anyone, I called dispatch." She'd tried to make her voice steady, as if giving a report to her boss. Which she was. But it was hard to keep the emotion out of it.

Duncan glanced at her pale yellow gown that in no way concealed, well, anything. It was thin and snug enough to show the outline of her breasts and baby bump.

Yes, definitely hard to keep the emotion out of this.

"I ran the plates," he told her. "The vehicle belongs to Alton Martinez in San Antonio."

She repeated the name to see if it rang any bells. It didn't. "Does he have a record?"

"I'll know in the next couple of minutes." Duncan stepped around her and went to the kitchen window to look out as she'd done.

He'd been in her house before but not in a while. Not since that night her father had died. In fact, Duncan had been here in her bed while her dad was being gunned down. Joelle knew she stood no chance of forgiving herself for that.

For years, Duncan and she had resisted the scalding attraction that'd been between them. They'd believed resisting was a necessity since they were fellow deputies, working side by side in sometimes dangerous situations. They hadn't wanted to risk a failed relationship that could have interfered with them doing their jobs. They'd resisted time after time, year after year. Until that night of her father's murder.

And it'd had disastrous consequences.

One good one, though, too.

Joelle hated she hadn't been with her father to try to stop his death, but she loved the baby she was carrying, and the pregnancy was the main reason she was managing to hold her life together. Duncan had helped some with the managing, too, by making sure they were on different shifts so she wouldn't have to see him that often. That's why it'd been such a jolt to have him respond to her call for help.

"Have you gotten any recent threats that I don't know about?" Duncan asked, the question yanking her out of her thoughts and forcing her to focus on the here and now.

"No. And I haven't made any recent arrests, either," she added, even though as sheriff, he would have already known that.

Of course, it wouldn't have to be anything recent to continue to be a threat. Sometimes, when criminals got out of jail, they went looking for anyone who'd had a part in their incarceration. No one immediately came to mind, though.

Duncan's phone dinged, and he tore his attention from the window to read the text he'd just gotten. "Martinez doesn't have a record, but about four hours ago, he reported his car stolen."

Joelle's chest clenched, and another wave of adrenaline washed through her. She had steeled herself up for the worst, but she'd hoped this would turn out to be nothing. The fact it was a stolen vehicle meant it was almost certainly something bad.

Staying on the other side of the window, she peered out, searching again for whatever sort of threat this might be. Her mind was having no trouble coming up with some awful scenarios. Especially one.

"Before I went to bed, I accessed some internet newspaper articles on my father's murder and my mother's disappearance," she told him.

No need for her to explain either of those incidents. Her father had been murdered, and on the same day, her mother, Sandra, had simply vanished. Both incidents had gutted her. Both had left her in desperate need of answers.

"I read any and every article connected to my parents," Joelle added to let Duncan know that wasn't anything out of the norm. "In one of them, a journalist mentioned that she was continuing to look into the murder and would post updates. I knew it was a long shot, that she probably didn't know anything we didn't, but in the comments, I asked if she'd found anything."

Duncan looked at her, their gazes connecting, and even in the dim light, she could see the sympathy in his eyes. Could practically hear the sigh that Joelle was certain he wanted to make.

"And you think...what...that your father's killer saw the comment and believed that maybe he or she wanted to stop you from digging?" he asked. He still didn't sigh. Nor did he dismiss it. "I saw the article. Saw the comment you posted."

Joelle figured she shouldn't have been surprised. Duncan felt guilty about her father's murder, too, and he was a cop just as she was. This was a crime they both wanted solved, and that meant digging through any and all possible leads.

"It's been five months," Duncan went on a moment later. "If the killer had planned on coming after one of us, you'd think that would have happened before now." He paused. "But the car was stolen, and the driver is nowhere in sight. So, I'm not writing anything off right now."

Good. Joelle had wanted him to take this seriously because she certainly was.

"We can work this a couple of ways," Duncan explained a moment later. "We can wait for the driver to show himself, or I can go ahead and call in every available deputy. We can flood the grounds with headlights and maybe spook the person enough for him or her to come out."

Joelle knew that no one in law enforcement wanted to be woken up at this hour, but her fellow cops, including the reserve deputies, would gladly come if they thought it meant catching her father's killer. Every member of the Saddle Ridge Sheriff's Office wanted justice for their former boss.

"Bring in the deputies," she advised. She glanced down at her gown again. "I'll hurry and change and then will keep watch at the front of the house."

Duncan made a sound of agreement, and while she hurried to her bedroom, she heard him call dispatch who in turn would contact the deputies. Since a few of them lived only a mile or so away, it shouldn't take long for them to start arriving.

Joelle wanted to believe that the extra help would mean a killer could be captured tonight. A capture that'd take place when she had plenty of backup so as to lessen the risk to her unborn child. But she had to stay grounded since this might not even be related to her father's death or her mother's disappearance.

Moving as fast as she could, Joelle pulled on a pair of maternity jeans, a loose top and her boots, and she hurried back into the living room. However, she came to a quick stop when she caught a whiff of something.

"Smoke," she heard Duncan say from the kitchen.

This time, the adrenaline came as a hard slam. Because Duncan was right. There was the faint scent of smoke in the air.

Duncan came barreling out of the kitchen and toward the front. "I don't see any signs of a fire in the back," he relayed to her as they both hurried to the living room window.

Joelle's heart was thudding now, and the fear came. A fire could be a ploy to get them out of the house. Or rather to get *her* out of the house. So she could be gunned down. But she didn't see flames anywhere.

"The scent's coming from here," Duncan muttered, glancing at the east wall of the living room.

The only windows on that particular side of the house were what was called clerestory, which meant they were above eye level and had been designed to let in natural light. That didn't stop Duncan. He dragged over a chair, anchoring it against the wall and hefted himself up to look out.

He cursed.

"There's a fire right next to your house," he told her, causing her heart to race even more. "It's already at least four feet high."

The exterior was wood, and while Joelle hoped it wouldn't easily ignite, her visitor must have believed that would be the result. Either that, or he or she had wanted Duncan and her just to go running out.

Duncan made another call to dispatch, this time to alert the fire department. Something the person outside must have figured they would do. And that meant the seconds were ticking down. If Duncan and she waited until the firefighters arrived, the house could be engulfed in flames, putting them and the baby at risk. But the risk could be there if they ran, too.

"My car's in the garage," she let him know.

The vehicle wasn't bullet resistant but then neither was Duncan's truck, which was parked by her porch. Still, if they were in her car, at least they could try to drive out of there if the fire overtook the house.

Duncan made another of those sounds of agreement, and he took her keys from her when she scooped them up from the foyer table. That meant he was no doubt planning on being behind the wheel and that he would insist she get down. The cop part of her hated she had to make such concessions. However, the baby changed her priorities, and Joelle knew that both Duncan and she would do anything and everything possible to keep their child safe.

"I have to disarm the security system until we're through the garage door," she relayed to him, using her phone to do that. The moment they were inside her car, though, she reset the alarm.

In the distance, Joelle heard the welcome sound of a cruiser's siren, but her relief over the backup was short-lived.

Because the next sound she heard was a blast.

Some kind of explosion roared through the house and garage, shaking the very foundation. Paint cans and gardening tools fell from the shelves and hooks, smashing onto the concrete floor. Each crash only escalated the urgency and fear.

So did the smoke.

The scent of it got much stronger, and Joelle could see whiffs of the smoke seeking beneath the mudroom door and into the garage. Thankfully, there was no smoke around the garage door itself, and that was likely the reason Duncan started the car and hit the remote on her visor to open the door.

"Stay down," he ordered her.

Joelle did. She strapped on her seat belt and sank down as low as she could. She also kept her gun ready in case she had to return fire.

Duncan threw the car into reverse and hit the accelerator, bolting out of the garage. Because of the way she was positioned, Joelle couldn't see the person responsible for the fire, but she had no doubts that Duncan was keeping watch.

The sirens got louder, and she saw the whirl of the blue lights slashing through the darkness. That would almost certainly get their attacker running. Or so she thought.

But she was wrong.

The bullet slammed into her windshield, crashing through the safety glass on the driver's side. For a heart-stopping second, she thought that Duncan had been hit, but he pressed even harder on the accelerator and got the car out of her driveway and onto the country road that fronted her house. He stopped just as the cruiser pulled in next to them.

"It's Luca," Duncan told her, referring to Deputy Luca Vanetti. "Text him and tell him to stay put until the others arrive. We have an active shooter. Tell him to let the other deputies know."

Joelle fired off a quick text, then braced herself for another shot. Or an explosion. Her house was burning, she was sure of that, but she couldn't deal with the sickening dread of losing her home and everything she owned. For now, she just had to focus on staying alive, and then she could figure out who was doing this.

And why.

She especially wanted to know the why in case that led her to her father's killer.

There was the sound of another siren. More whirling lights. Two more vehicles arriving on scene. What didn't happen was another round of gunfire, which meant the shooter was likely already on the run. Joelle prayed, though, that someone would spot the person.

Because she was so focused on listening for their attacker, Joelle gasped when the sound shot through the car. But it wasn't a bullet. It was her phone, and Joelle saw a familiar name on the screen. Molly Radel, a former deputy who'd transferred to working as a dispatcher after she got pregnant. Even though Molly was on leave, awaiting the birth of her baby, it was possible she'd been called in to assist in some way.

"Molly," Joelle answered, and she was about to give the woman a quick explanation as to what was going on, but Molly spoke before Joelle could do that.

"You have to help me," Molly said, her voice trembling and frantic. "Someone's breaking into my house."

The words had no sooner left Molly's mouth when Jo-elle heard the woman scream.

Chapter Two

Even though Joelle hadn't put the call on speaker, Duncan heard the woman's scream loud and clear. Since Joelle had greeted Molly by name, he also had no trouble figuring out that something was seriously wrong.

"Put the phone on speaker," Duncan told Joelle, and the moment she'd done that, he tried to figure out what the heck was going on. "Molly?" he asked.

He could hear what he thought were the sounds of a struggle, but the dispatcher didn't answer. And that caused Duncan to curse. He had every available lawman responding to the situation here at Joelle's. A situation that might escalate even more if the attacker continued to shoot at them. But Duncan knew he had to go to Molly, and he had to do that now.

"Use my phone to let the deputies know that I'm heading to Molly's place," Duncan relayed to Joelle. "I want Luca to follow us as backup."

Of course, that meant he'd be taking Joelle with him since there wasn't time for him to get her safely into a cruiser. He got confirmation of that when he heard Molly scream again. The woman was obviously fighting for her life, and there wasn't a second to lose.

Duncan gunned the engine to get them out of there,

and he kept watch around them as he headed for the road. Thankfully, no shots came their way. That was the good news. The bad news was that could mean the shooter had stopped firing so he could go in pursuit of them.

Joelle finished a quick call to Luca to request backup and then went back to her own phone. "Molly?" she tried again.

The sounds of the struggle had stopped. No more screams. Nothing. And that tightened every muscle in Duncan's body. Hell. The sounds of her screams had been terrifying, but the silence was even worse. Because the screams meant she'd at least been alive.

He thought back to the petite, young brunette who'd been a dispatcher for about six months now. She was pregnant, and she wasn't married but had instead opted for artificial insemination to have a child. Molly's parents were dead, and since she had no siblings, she would almost certainly be alone. It was info that everyone in town knew, and it was possible that someone had used that particular info to go after her.

But why?

"This can't be a coincidence," Joelle muttered, taking the words right out of Duncan's mouth.

Yeah, Duncan was leaning that direction as well. Two pregnant women attacked on the same night in the same small town. That would, indeed, be one hell of a coincidence if the incidents weren't related. Still, it was possible that there were two forces at work here. Duncan just didn't know exactly what those two forces were right now, but he'd need to find out and fast.

When there was an attack or kidnapping involving a pregnant woman, it was usually connected to some kind of domestic dispute. In fact, the number one threat to a pregnant woman was being murdered or seriously injured by the woman's partner. But there were also those crimes that involved kidnapping or killing a pregnant woman so the baby could be taken. With Molly so close to giving birth, that was definitely a motive at the top of Duncan's list.

But that didn't explain the attack on Joelle.

She was in her fifth month of pregnancy. Still a long way from delivering their child. A kidnapper would have to hold her for months. Not exactly a comforting thought, but then none of this was anywhere near comfortable.

Duncan cranked up the speed when he reached the road and headed toward town. Since he'd known Molly his whole life, he knew where she lived and didn't have to look up her address. He just drove and tried to figure out how to make this trip as safe as possible for Joelle.

A safety she likely wouldn't want if she was thinking like a cop.

But if necessary, he'd need to remind her that she was on desk duty until the baby arrived. That wasn't a personal preference on his part simply because she was carrying his child. It was standard practice in the sheriff's office, and it was something her father would have insisted on had he still been alive.

Beside him, Joelle continued to try to get some kind of response from Molly by calling out the woman's name into her phone. Molly didn't answer. But there was a response in the form of a dead line. When she tried to call again and got the same thing, Duncan knew that someone had switched off the phone.

"I'll call dispatch to have Molly's phone tracked," Joelle told him.

He could hear the fear and nerves in every word she'd spoken. Fear that was there for a reason because they both knew that whoever was attacking Molly could have also disabled the phone, making it untraceable. Duncan hoped like the devil that hadn't happened, though, because if Molly wasn't home, the phone would be their best bet in tracking her.

Thankfully, there was no other traffic on the rural road at this hour so Duncan continued to press on the accelerator, eating up the distance between Joelle's and Molly's. Luca stayed right behind him in the cruiser.

Duncan's phone rang, and when he saw Deputy Ronnie Bishop's name on the screen, he took the call on speaker. "Is everyone all right?" Duncan immediately asked since he knew Ronnie was at Joelle's.

"So far," Ronnie quickly assured him. "No signs of the shooter, though, and there's been no gunfire since Joelle and you left. No one's attempted to get to the stolen black car, either."

If the gunman had, indeed, been coming after Joelle and him, that would mean he or she had a second vehicle. And likely a partner. Either that or the gunman had positioned a second vehicle earlier and then driven the stolen one to Joelle's. Duncan couldn't think of a good motive for a would-be killer to do that, but the reason could be a clue to who had attacked them and why.

"How many deputies are there?" Duncan asked Ronnie.

"Six, including me. The fire department is here, too, but they're holding off until they get the word from you that it's safe to try to put out the fire."

It wasn't safe. Not with a gunman, maybe two, in the area. Hell, there could be even more than that if this was some kind of coordinated attack. No way could Duncan risk the lives of his deputies and the firemen when Joelle wasn't even there. Yes, she might lose her house to the fire, but the goal was to get everyone out of this alive and then catch the SOB responsible.

"Everyone stays in their vehicles for now," Duncan instructed, "but have two of the deputies go to the end of Joelle's road and keep watch for anyone trying to sneak away from there. Two more should stay put in case the shooter isn't done. Send the other two to Molly's."

If Molly had been kidnapped, or worse, then Duncan figured he was going to need as much help as possible.

Ronnie gave a fast assurance that he'd do as Duncan asked, and they ended the call just as Duncan finally made it to the turn to Molly's. It wasn't a typical subdivision or neighborhood like in a city but rather a spattering of homes that had been built on multi-acre lots. With all the trees and natural landscape, it was more like living in the country, which made for a peaceful lifestyle.

It also meant Molly's neighbors might not have been able to see or hear what was going on.

Added to that, Duncan was well aware that her nearest neighbors were all senior citizens. That was the reason he hadn't called any of them to go check on Molly and try to stop whatever was happening. Duncan hadn't wanted to risk any of them being hurt or killed. This was definitely a situation for law enforcement.

"I want you to stay down," Duncan told Joelle, and he made sure it sounded like the order it was.

She didn't protest. Not with words, anyway. But he knew this was eating away at her. Especially since someone was threatening and maybe had already harmed someone she knew well.

Duncan sped into Molly's driveway, his gaze immediately firing all around. There were no vehicles in front of the house. Nor was there anyone in sight. Just the darkness and the milky yellow illumination coming from the porch light.

"The front door's open," Joelle murmured.

It was. Duncan had noticed that right away, but he aimed a quick scowl at Joelle to let her know if she had seen that, then it meant she wasn't staying down. Joelle muttered some profanity and slipped lower into the seat.

With Luca's cruiser squealing to a stop behind him, Duncan hurried out of the car, and while keeping watch, he ran toward the porch. He couldn't risk sitting around, waiting to see if he could figure out what was going on because at this exact moment, Molly could be inside fighting for her life.

Duncan barreled up the porch steps, taking them two at a time, and pinned his focus to the open door. If Molly's attacker was still in there, he had to be prepared in case the guy shot at him. That's why Duncan tried to listen for any sounds of a struggle or movement.

He heard nothing.

And knew that wasn't a good sign. Ditto for what he spotted on the porch just to the right side of the welcome mat.

Drops of blood.

Duncan was sure that's what it was, and cursing, he stepped around the drops and went inside. Of course, just his mere presence could contaminate the scene, but again, Molly was the priority here. He had to hold out hope that the blood belonged to her attacker, that Molly had somehow managed to fight him off and sent the SOB running.

"Molly?" he called out.

No need for him to stay quiet since there was no element of surprise here. If the attacker was still inside the house, he would have heard the car that Duncan had been driving and the cruiser. Molly would have, too, and that meant if she'd been capable of calling out for help, she likely would have already done it.

Trying to steel himself for the worst but praying for the best, Duncan went into the house, staying low and leading with his gun. His attention whipped to the right, then the left. He took in the toppled lamp on the floor, but it seemed to be the only sign of a struggle.

Room by room, he made his way through the place, recalling the time or two he'd been here with his folks when they'd visited Molly's parents. Years ago, even before Molly had been born. Duncan was thirty-seven and Molly just twenty-four so he'd been plenty old enough to recall coming here for her folks to show off their baby girl. Maybe that was one of the reasons Molly had wanted to raise her child here. Her home. A place where she'd no doubt felt safe.

That last thought twisted his gut into knots so Duncan kept moving, kept searching, all the while listening for, well, anything. In addition to being able to hear anything in the house, he also needed to make sure nothing was going on outside with Joelle and Luca. So far, he wasn't hearing or seeing anything. Nothing out of place except for that lamp.

Until he made it to one of the bedrooms.

Molly's no doubt, and there were plenty of signs of a struggle here. The bed was empty, but the covers had been dragged off, and the clock and lamp that'd almost certainly been on the nightstand were now on the floor.

"Molly?" he called out again and still got no response.

The overhead light was off, but there was a nightlight plugged in the outlet near the door to the adjoining bath. It was enough for him to see more of those blood drops.

Hell.

Duncan moved faster now, checking out the bathroom for any signs of Molly. Nothing. So he kept moving, hurry-

ing to the other rooms. They were all empty, but he got another jolt when he saw the nursery all decked out in shades
of pink. Since Joelle's and his baby was also a girl, it made
the gut punch even harder.

Pushing that aside, he made his way back through the
house and was careful not to touch anything. Whoever had
taken Molly might have left prints or some kind of trace
evidence in the struggle, and Duncan didn't want to compromise that any more than he already had.

He went back to the porch and saw that Luca was out of
the cruiser and near Joelle's vehicle. The deputy immediately looked up at him, but Duncan had to shake his head.

"Molly's not here," Duncan relayed to them. "And there's
blood on the porch and in the master bedroom. I want a
BOLO for Molly and a CSI team in here right away."

That got Joelle coming out of the car. "There's a garden
shed in the back," she said, already moving as if to head
in that direction. "Molly could be in there."

Duncan cursed and went after her. "I know about the shed
and was about to check it out." He was about to order her back
to the car, but she spoke before he could manage to say it.

"I have to help," she insisted.

Joelle wasn't crying. She was too much of a cop for that.
But her voice was shaky, and he figured that applied to the
rest of her as well. Along with the mother lode of adrenaline, she was also battling the overwhelming fear that a
woman they both knew had been kidnapped or killed and
that the same thing had nearly happened to her.

"Stay close to me," Duncan finally agreed.

He'd make this search quick so he could get Joelle into
at least some minimal cover. Then, he could take her to
the sheriff's office while they regrouped and figured out
their next move.

As he'd remembered, the shed was in the backyard, not far from the porch that wrapped around the entire house. Duncan made a cursory look of the area, then a quick glance into the shed just to see if by some miracle Molly was hiding there. She wasn't.

"Molly?" he called out one last time.

When he got no response, he hurried back to the car with Joelle and got her inside. "Start calling her neighbors," Duncan instructed. "I want to know if anyone saw or heard anything."

He doubted that'd been the case, though. If so, those neighbors would have already headed over. Still, it was possible that someone had heard something that would give them clues as to who had taken Molly.

There was the howl of sirens in the distance, and Duncan knew it wouldn't be long before more deputies arrived. Good. He'd have them check around the place while he got on the phone with the Texas Rangers and Highway Patrol. Both agencies would get word of the BOLO, but Duncan wanted to emphasize that Molly was pregnant and she worked for law enforcement. Molly was one of them, and that would hopefully get her the highest priority.

Duncan took out his phone, ready to get started on those calls, but he stopped when he caught some movement from the corner of his eye. He pivoted in that direction, in the same motion taking aim with his Glock. Then, he stopped when he spotted something.

The woman walking toward them.

Correction: staggering toward them.

It wasn't Molly. No, this woman was older and had graying black hair that was tangled around her face. She was barefoot and wearing a ripped shirt over stained gray yoga pants.

Duncan's first thought was this was Sandra McCullough, Joelle's mother who'd deserted her family the day her husband had been murdered. No one had seen or heard from her since. But it wasn't Sandra, and Duncan had no idea who she was.

Joelle got out of the car, taking aim as well. So did Luca, but Duncan could see both of the woman's hands, and she wasn't armed. Still, this could be some kind of ploy so he approached her with caution.

"Who are you?" Duncan demanded. "Are you hurt?" He didn't see any signs of injury, but it was possible some of the stains on her clothes were dried blood.

"I'm sorry," the woman said as she came even closer.

That put some ice in his veins. "Sorry for what?" And because it had to be asked, he added. "Are you the one who took Molly?"

She didn't answer but rather just kept walking, her feet dragging through the yard. Her eyes looked vacant. Robotic, even. As if someone had forgotten to turn on a switch. Duncan was betting she'd either been drugged or was in shock.

"This is all my fault," the woman muttered. Her voice was flat and barely a whisper. "Everything that's happening is my fault." She dropped to her knees, her gaze shifting to Joelle. "I'm so sorry, but he wants you dead."

A hoarse sob tore from her throat, and the woman collapsed into a heap on the ground.

Chapter Three

While Joelle sat in the waiting room of the emergency room of Saddle Ridge Hospital, she tried to keep her breathing level and tamp down the worry that was threatening to cloud her mind. Worry wouldn't help—not her baby, not Molly and not her. What she needed right now was for Molly to be found alive and well and for her to find answers as to what the heck was going on.

Duncan was clearly after those answers, too, and he had been on the phone nonstop since they'd arrived at the hospital with the mystery woman. The woman who'd delivered that sickening message.

I'm so sorry, but he wants you dead.

That was definitely something Joelle hadn't wanted to hear, and it'd left her with even more questions. Who was the woman and who was the *he* she'd proclaimed wanted to kill her? Was he the person who'd driven that stolen car to her house and set the fire? It was hard for her to believe that it wasn't connected, but until the woman regained consciousness, all Joelle could do was speculate and deal with her own phone calls. So far, none of those calls had given her any good news.

Plenty of bad, though.

Her house was basically in ashes now because the fire

department hadn't been able to move in to try to save it since there'd been the threat of an active shooter. There were no signs of the shooter now, though. No sign of Molly, either. And the now-unconscious mystery woman had had no ID on her so they didn't even know who she was.

However, Joelle had gotten some good news, not from a call but rather the checkup she'd had shortly after Duncan and she had arrived at the hospital. Despite the traumatic situation she'd experienced, the baby was fine. The monitors had shown a strong, steady heartbeat and lots of movement—signs that had fulfilled a lot of Joelle's prayers. Her baby was okay.

Now, Joelle had to make sure she stayed that way.

The only instructions the doctor had given her was to get some rest, and Duncan had been there to hear that part. Which meant he'd soon be trying to get her off her feet. She was exhausted, no doubt about that, and exhaustion wasn't good for the baby, but neither was having shots fired at them. To make sure an attack like that didn't happen again, they needed answers fast.

Since Duncan was still on the phone, Joelle went after some of those answers by making a call to dispatch to check if there'd been any missing persons' reports in the area of someone matching their mystery woman's description. There hadn't been, but Joelle had known that was a long shot, that the woman could have come from anywhere and maybe wasn't missing at all. She could have arrived shortly before she'd staggered toward Joelle's house.

Emphasis on *staggered*.

She hadn't been steady on her feet at all and seemed dazed, perhaps even drugged. But it was also possible she had been experiencing some kind of medical emergency that had created those symptoms. If so, the woman might not have even been aware of what she was saying.

I'm so sorry, but he wants you dead.

Though she certainly hadn't seemed so dazed or drugged when she'd spoken those words. She'd seemed adamant about delivering a warning with a potential deadly outcome.

Joelle was about to text one of the deputies to see if there'd been any signs of a vehicle that the woman could have used to get to or near her place, but before she could press the number, she got an incoming call from one of her brothers, Ruston McCullough, a homicide detective with San Antonio PD.

It wasn't Ruston's first call of the morning. That initial one had come while Duncan and she were en route to the hospital. She had assured Ruston and her other brother, Slater, and their kid sister, Bree, that she hadn't been harmed, but Joelle knew they were worried about her. Knew, too, that the calls to check on her would continue until they could see her face-to-face and make sure the baby and she were, indeed, okay.

"Anything?" Ruston immediately asked. His tone was brusque as it usually was, but Joelle was aware that the question covered a lot of bases, including her own state of mind.

"No. We're still in limbo when it comes to any info that'll help." She paused, had to because of the sudden lump in her throat. "Still nothing on Molly. Someone took her, and she has to be terrified."

Joelle refused to believe it could be worse than that. She wouldn't accept that Molly could be hurt or dead. She had to cling to the hope they would somehow find her and bring her safely home.

"Any ransom demand?" Ruston questioned.

Joelle had to repeat her "no." But in a way, a ransom demand would be a positive sign. It meant she'd been taken for money and would presumably be released unharmed if the money was paid.

Ruston sighed and paused a long time. "I'm sorry about your house. You've got the keys and security code to stay at my place, but I don't want you there alone. Just hang with Duncan until I can get there. I want to keep coordinating with the Rangers to try to locate Molly."

"Keep on that," she insisted. She would have also told him she would come up with a safe place to stay, however, when Duncan ended his latest call and started her way, she put the rest of this conversation on hold. "I have to go," she told Ruston. "I'll let you know if I get any updates."

She ended the call and stood to face Duncan. He definitely didn't look to be the bearer of good news, and that caused her heart to sink again. She prayed he wasn't about to tell her Molly was dead.

"We haven't found Molly yet," Duncan immediately said, probably picking up the worst-case-scenario vibe from her expression. "Some of the reserve deputies are canvasing the area around her house to find out if anyone saw anything."

The late hour wouldn't help with that, but maybe Molly had managed to scream or something. If so, that would have already been reported, but Joelle had to hang on to the hope that they'd get a viable lead.

"The CSIs are going through Molly's house and the stolen car left at your place," Duncan continued. "They're still looking for her vehicle, too." Even though it wasn't necessary for him to identify what *her* he was referring to, he tipped his head to the exam room where the medical staff had taken the mystery woman. "She didn't have any ID on her."

"And there's no missing person's report matching her description," Joelle provided.

Duncan nodded. "Apparently, she drifted in and out of consciousness when she was in the ambulance so when we're able to speak to her, she might be able to tell us who she is. And why she issued that warning," he tacked onto that.

Yes, that was vital for the safety of their baby, and Joelle reminded herself that there were a lot of people working to get answers and make sure that *safety* happened.

"Do you think this woman and the warning are directly connected to Molly?" Joelle came out and asked.

Duncan's gaze locked with hers. Something they usually avoided because of the heat that was always there between them. Heat that came despite any and everything going on. There'd always be an intimate connection, especially now that she was carrying his child, but because she was so worried about Molly, it was easier for Joelle to shove that heat aside.

"Yes," he admitted. The sigh he added was long, heavy and weary. "That's why I made a call to the FBI. I wanted to see if they were aware of any black market baby rings or perpetrators in the area who could be targeting pregnant women. Nothing like that is on their radar, but they're checking to see if this is someone from out of state."

Joelle had tried to maintain a stoic expression, her cop face. She tried not to let the possibility of something like that give her this jolt of fear. But it did. Mercy, it did.

Duncan muttered some profanity and took hold of her arm. Probably because she looked ready to collapse. Joelle was almost certain that wouldn't happen, almost, but she allowed him to help her back into one of the chairs, and he sank down on the one beside her.

"Deep breaths," he advised her. "Count to ten. Tell me the latest names you're considering for the baby."

Part of her resented Duncan for seeing the weakness in her and knowing she needed help. Part of her also resented that such measures might be necessary to keep herself from spiraling. But the resentment was really for herself, for feeling this clawing terror all the way to the bone. Those sort of emotions didn't help. In fact, they could hurt, and she didn't want anything else that could hinder them in this investigation.

"I'll be all right," she muttered, hoping it was true.

The sound Duncan made let her know that he wasn't so sure of that at all, and she might have launched into more attempts at convincing him if her phone hadn't rang. "It's my sister again," she muttered, and even though Joelle wasn't in the mood to talk to her, she had to answer it or it would cause Bree to worry even more than she was already was.

"Bree," Joelle greeted. "I'm all right."

"So you say." Her sister's sigh was plenty loud enough for Joelle to hear. "I'll believe it when I see it. I'm coming home, but I can't get there for at least a couple of days."

Joelle groaned. Bree was a lawyer working on a special task force in Dallas, six hours away, and she knew Bree had used all her vacation time and then some when she'd come home after their father's murder and disappearance. Since Joelle figured she stood no chance whatsoever of convincing Bree she was fine and didn't need her sister to be there, she went with a different tactic.

"Everyone in the sheriff's office is tied up with the investigation," Joelle spelled out. "And right now Saddle Ridge isn't the safest place to be."

"I'm coming home," Bree insisted, and then she paused. Sighed again. "I need to see you. There are things I want to talk to you about."

Joelle didn't like the sound of that, especially since she and her sister communicated at least weekly either by phone call or text. "Is something wrong?" Joelle came out and asked.

It was a valid question. Like her, Bree had been devastated with what had happened to their parents. Added to that, Bree had broken up with her longtime boyfriend, Luca. Then again, Luca and Bree had had an on-again, off-again thing going on since high school. Since Bree was often involved in high-profile legal cases for the state and was gone a lot, both Luca and she had had other relationships. But something had happened between Luca and Bree to make her sister pull the plug and now things were permanently off.

Or so Bree had said.

Luca wasn't offering up anything so Joelle wasn't sure what had happened. Maybe it was something similar to what had gone on between Duncan and her. Too much pain and grief. Too much guilt. Too much, period.

"I should be home by early next week," Bree added a moment later. "In the meantime, you stay safe. I love you, Joelle."

"I'll certainly try," Joelle assured her. "And I love you, too," she said, ending the call just as the door to the exam room finally opened.

It wasn't the mystery woman who came out, of course, but it was a familiar face. Dr. Chase Benton, one of the doctors who worked at Saddle Ridge General Hospital.

Dr. Benton spotted them and walked their way as Duncan and she headed to him. "Is she awake?" Duncan immediately asked.

"She is, for the moment anyway," the doctor said, but there was caution in his voice. He stepped in front of Duncan when he started toward the exam room. "I'm well aware that you need to see her," he quickly added. "I've heard what's going on, and I understand you have to question her, but you should know that she's still unable to stay awake for more than a couple of seconds. Unable to tell me her name as well. I suspect she's been drugged, and that the drugs combined with a head injury are the reasons she's lapsing in and out of consciousness."

That wasn't a surprise to either Duncan or her, and that led them to more questions. Who'd drugged her and why? Hopefully, they'd know the answers to that soon.

"Her blood pressure is high as well," the doctor continued. "And that means when you question her, you can't push too hard. I can't give her anything right now for the blood pressure until I find out what other drugs are in her system."

Duncan groaned. "I have to push," he insisted. "Molly Radel and her baby's life could depend on it."

Dr. Benton's eyes widened. "You believe the patient had something to do with that?"

"I think the likelihood is high that there's a connection. It's possible the woman can tell us who took Molly."

Despite Duncan's use of *likelihood* and *possible*, the doctor nodded and stepped to the side. "All right, you can question her, but I have to be there. And trust me, I will pull the plug on the interview if I feel she can't handle it."

Duncan nodded, too, while he was already on the move. With Dr. Benton and Joelle right behind him, Duncan stepped into the ER room where the woman was lying on the bed. She was hooked up to a monitor and had an IV in the back of her hand. Joelle also spotted some injuries.

There was a gash on the side of her head, some bruising as well and her feet were covered with cuts and scrapes.

"She obviously walked barefoot through some rough terrain," the doctor pointed out. "There was also powder on her clothes. The kind of powder you'd get from a deployed airbag."

So maybe she'd been involved in a car accident. However, that didn't explain what had happened to her shoes or why she'd ended up walking to Molly's. Or the ominous message she'd delivered.

The woman's eyes were open, and when she lifted her head, her attention went straight to them. Joelle didn't see any recognition in her expression, only wariness and confusion. Added to that, her gaze still had that dazed look she'd had when she arrived at Molly's.

"I'm Sheriff Duncan Holder," he said, stepping closer to her. He tipped his head to Joelle. "And this is Deputy Joelle McCullough. Could you tell us your name?"

The woman looked at the doctor and then shifted her attention to Joelle. "I came to see you," she muttered, her voice a ragged whisper.

That gave Joelle some hope. If the woman remembered that, then she might recall other things, too.

"You did," Joelle verified. She started to remind her of what she'd said before she collapsed but decided to press for an ID instead. "Who are you?"

She shook her head as if trying to figure that out, and then murmured. "Kate Moreland."

Duncan got out his phone as she spoke the last syllable, and he fired off a quick text, no doubt to get someone at the sheriff's office to run a background check on her.

"Kate Moreland," Joelle repeated, mentally testing out the name, but it didn't ring any bells. "You know me?"

Kate shook her head. "I know of you." Her voice broke into a hoarse groan. She eased back onto the bed and closed her eyes. "I had to warn you."

Another positive sign that she'd remembered that. Of course, the warning she'd delivered hadn't been positive at all.

"You said someone wanted me dead," Joelle reminded her. "Who?"

She didn't open her eyes, and it was at least fifteen seconds before she answered. "My son," she finally said, and she broke down into a heaving sob. A reaction that caused the numbers on the monitor to spike.

"You need to leave," Dr. Benton insisted. "Her blood pressure's too high. Step out while I try to get her stabilized." It wasn't a request, and the doctor practically muscled them out of the room.

Duncan cursed and took out his phone. "Slater's running the background check on her. I'll see if he's got anything yet." However, Duncan's phone rang before he could call her brother.

"It's Ronnie," he relayed to her, and he put the deputy's call on speaker.

"We found a car, a dark blue Audi," Ronnie said right off. "It looks as if the driver hit the east side of the bridge and lost control. It was off the road and all the way down on the banks of the creek."

The creek was only about a half mile from Molly's, and if it did, indeed, belong to Kate, then the woman had likely been traveling from the interstate. If she'd been coming from town, then the collision would have probably happened on the west side of the bridge. Also, if she'd been coming from town, Duncan or one of the responding deputies would have spotted her on the road before she'd made it to Molly's.

"I'm running the plates now," Ronnie continued. "But there was a purse and a phone in the vehicle. According to the driver's license, the purse's owner is Kate Moreland. She has a San Antonio address."

San Antonio was a half hour away, which meant Ruston could no doubt help with getting them any info they needed on her. And her son. Joelle wanted to know his name and why Kate had believed he might want to kill her.

"When you do a thorough search of the car," Duncan said, "check her GPS to confirm if she was heading to Molly's or Joelle's. And let me know if you find anything we can use."

Ronnie assured him that he would, and Duncan ended the call to make one to Slater. Her brother answered on the first ring.

"Kate Moreland," Slater immediately said, and he rattled off an address in San Antonio. "Age fifty-three. Divorced. No criminal record. She's a very wealthy businesswoman who owns a half dozen martial arts and workout gyms."

"You have the name of her son?" Duncan pressed.

"Yeah. Brad. Age twenty-eight, and I'm just scratching the surface on him. Why? Is he part of this?"

"Kate seems to think so," Duncan quickly verified. "She believes her son might be out to kill Joelle."

Slater cursed. "He's got a record for assault during a bar fight, but I don't see any connection to Joelle or Saddle Ridge…" His words trailed off, and he cursed again. "But his ex-wife, Shanda Cantrell, does. My dad and you arrested her nearly two years ago for reckless driving and resisting arrest. Either of you remember that?"

"I do," Duncan said.

"So do I," Joelle murmured, trying to zoom in on any info that was lingering around in her memory. The info had plenty of gaps in it so she took out her phone and started searching while she continued. "I recall Dad and Duncan bringing in a woman for those charges. They had me search her for weapons, and because she was being so combative, Dad put her in a holding cell."

"A definite yes to her being combative," Duncan agreed. "She tried to take a punch at me. And she cursed and spat at Joelle. Cursed the sheriff, too."

Slater must have pulled up the file right before she did because he was the one to add more. "She ended up pleading guilty, paid a fine and did some community service. Dad worked it out so she could do that service in San Antonio so she wouldn't miss any work at her job as a florist." Slater paused a moment. "Had she been drinking?" he asked. "Was that the reason for the reckless driving?"

"No alcohol," Joelle was able to provide. "She admitted to having been in a heated argument with someone on her phone. She was also speeding when she rammed into a mailbox, swerved and nearly hit another car." Then, she paused. Had to. Because she spotted something in the file notes. "Shanda was three months pregnant."

Both Duncan and Slater went silent, but she could hear Slater clicking away on a keyboard. "She has no children listed. Neither does Brad."

So either Shanda had miscarried or the baby had died. Either way, that might play into motive. If there was motive for Shanda, that is. Kate hadn't said a word about her ex-daughter-in-law, only her son. Maybe then, losing a child had something to do with why Kate had come here to issue that warning about Brad.

"I'll obviously want a conversation with both Shanda and Brad," Duncan insisted.

"I can arrange that," Slater volunteered. "When I call him, how much do you want him to know about his mother?"

Duncan's forehead bunched up while he gave that some thought. Joelle definitely wanted to hear how he was going to handle this, but her phone rang, and her chest tightened when she saw *Unknown Caller* on the screen.

"This could be the ransom demand," Joelle muttered, answering the call on speaker and hitting the record function on her phone.

She steeled herself up to hear a snarled threat and demand from the kidnapper. But it wasn't.

"Help me," the woman said.

It was Molly.

Chapter Four

"I'll have to call you back," Duncan told Slater the moment he heard Molly's voice.

He didn't wait for Slater to respond. Duncan ended the call and went closer to Joelle.

"Where are you?" Joelle asked Molly. "Are you all right?"

Molly didn't answer, but Duncan could hear some kind of shuffling around, and several moments later, someone spoke. But this time, it wasn't Molly.

"Don't ask any questions," a man said. His voice was muffled and practically a growl. No doubt because he was trying to disguise it. Did that mean Duncan knew this person? "I made a mistake, and I'm trying to fix it."

Despite the man demanding no questions, Duncan had so many of them. Joelle no doubt did, too. But at the top of their list had to be if Molly had been harmed.

"We're listening," Duncan prompted so the man would continue.

"A big mistake," he muttered, adding some profanity. "I'll leave the woman somewhere you can find her."

Duncan jumped right on that. It wasn't the ransom demand—or any other kind of demand—he'd been expecting. "Where?"

"I'll call you once I've dropped her off, tell you where

she is, and you can come and get her," the man was quick to say.

Of course, that meant the guy would probably be long gone by the time they arrived to get Molly. But this could also be a trap to draw Joelle and him out.

"Is Molly all right?" Duncan asked, hoping that Molly would be able to answer that for herself.

"She's shaken up but fine. Like I said, taking her was a mistake."

Duncan wanted to press for more. He wanted to know why kidnapping Molly had been a mistake. Had this been a case of the wrong person being taken? Had Joelle been the target? He needed answers to all of that, but he especially wanted to know whose blood was in the house and on Molly's porch. If it was Molly's, then she was more than just shaken up.

"Leave Molly somewhere now," Duncan bargained. "She and her baby need to be checked by a doctor."

Silence. For a long time. And Duncan hoped like the devil that the guy was considering that. The sooner they got Molly, the better.

"I'll call you when I call you," the man finally snarled, and he ended the conversation before Duncan could say anything else.

Duncan immediately cursed and tried to call the kidnapper back. It wasn't a surprise, though, when the guy didn't answer. Still, Duncan reminded himself that the call was a positive sign. Molly was alive, and the man who'd taken her wanted to return her.

Supposedly.

He cursed again and looked at Joelle. "He could be using Molly and her baby as bait," she muttered.

"Yeah." But Duncan didn't need to spell out the rest.

He'd have to go to Molly even if a trap was a high proba-bility. Which it was. He'd have to go even if there was only a slim chance they'd get Molly back.

"You'll take backup," Joelle said, proving that they were thinking the same thing. "And you'll be careful."

Duncan shouldn't have felt good about her adding that last part. But he did. There'd been so many weeks of ten-sion between Joelle and him. So much guilt. Now, though, they were on the same side again, and he realized just how much he'd missed this. He'd had a thing for her for years, that wasn't going away, but he missed working with her almost as much as he missed being with her.

Almost.

He glanced up the hall when he saw someone approach-ing, and his body braced. But it wasn't a threat. It was Luca who'd gone back to Joelle's after he'd escorted Duncan and her to the hospital.

"No sign of the gunman yet," Luca reported. "No other shots fired after you left the scene. How are you two? Were either of you hurt?"

"We're fine," Joelle assured him. "We just got a call from the kidnapper." She handed him her phone. "The re-cording of the conversation is on there, but the kidnapper claims he intends to return Molly."

That put some hope in Luca's intense brown eyes. Hope that disappeared as fast as it'd come. "You believe him?"

"Too soon to tell," Duncan muttered.

Luca's phone rang. "It's the fire department," he ex-plained. "I'd better take this." He stepped away to do that, and Duncan turned back to Joelle.

"When the kidnapper does call back, you won't be going with me to pick up Molly," he told her.

Her mouth tightened, but she didn't argue. She had to

know if this was a trap, then she was likely the intended target.

Well, maybe she was.

"You don't resemble Molly," he said, thinking out loud. "You live miles from each other. Yes, you're both pregnant, and she's a former cop, but that's about it."

Joelle nodded. "Maybe it wasn't about mistaking Molly for me but he could possibly see the kidnapping as a mistake. It's possible he didn't know she was pregnant." She paused. "Or he could have just changed his mind."

That was true, but it still didn't explain the attack on Joelle. Or maybe it did. "If someone wanted to kidnap pregnant women, there could have been two teams operating. The one that hit your place and the one that went after Molly."

Joelle made a sound of agreement but wasn't able to add anything else because the door to Kate Moreland's room opened, and Dr. Benton came out.

Benton was quick to shake his head. "You won't be able to speak to Ms. Moreland for at least a couple of hours. Maybe longer. Her blood pressure isn't stable, and she's at risk for a hypertension crisis, which could lead to a stroke or heart attack. I'll give you a call when it's safe for her to have visitors."

Duncan couldn't press to continue the interview, not when it could put the woman's life in danger. But there were also more pressing dangers than Ms. Moreland's health.

"Ms. Moreland was worried about her son, Brad," Duncan told the doctor. "She thought he might want to harm Joelle in some way. That's why she was heading to Joelle's place, but she was near Molly's when she was involved in a car crash."

A crash that might or might not have been an accident.

That was yet something else Duncan would need to find out about.

"If she's right about her son, he could be dangerous," Duncan went on. "I'll keep Deputy Vanetti standing guard outside her room now," he added, motioning to Luca who was only a few feet away and still on the phone. "And I'll get a reserve deputy in to replace him." That's because Duncan needed all his best trained deputies on the investigation.

The doctor nodded and gave an uneasy glance around. "I'll alert security, too, that there could be a potential problem."

Security was basically one guard who monitored the cameras positioned in and around the hospital. Duncan didn't know who was on duty tonight, but a deputy would be the best bet to keep Kate safe.

"I'll contact a reserve deputy," Luca volunteered after the doctor had walked away, already on his phone. No doubt to call security. "And I'll get the hospital guard a photo of Brad Moreland so he can keep an eye out for him."

"Good idea," Duncan told him and added a thanks before he got Joelle moving.

"You want me to walk with you to the exit?" Luca asked.

It was tempting, but he had to shake his head. "Best to stay on Kate's door. But I will use your cruiser."

It was bullet-resistant and parked right outside the ER. A safer way to get Joelle to the sheriff's office than using her car.

Luca immediately handed over the keys, and while Joelle and Duncan started down the hall, she typed out a text. "To Slater," she explained. "I want to fill him in about what's going on."

Good idea because Slater and all the other deputies needed to know about Kate and her son. About Shanda as well. Even though they didn't have any direct proof, the attacks on Joelle and Molly might, indeed, be related to Shanda's arrest two years ago. That was a long time to wait to act out on a grudge, and that's why they had to learn everything they could about the woman.

Duncan stopped at the ER doors and peered out into the parking lot. He didn't see any immediate threat. In fact, because of the early hour, there wasn't anyone around.

No one visible, anyway.

Of course, there was always the threat that a gunman had positioned himself to wait for them to come out. And that's why Duncan had to test the waters. Something Joelle wasn't going to like. The cruiser was close, but he wanted it as close to the ER doors as possible. That would minimize Joelle's time for being out in the open where she'd be an easy target.

"Wait here," he instructed.

Nope, she didn't like it, but she didn't voice her objection. However, she did take out her gun and started glancing around to make sure he wasn't about to be ambushed.

Duncan also took out his weapon and hurried to the cruiser. He kept an eye on Joelle as well because if she was a target, then an attacker could use this opportunity to go after her. But he held out hope that Molly's kidnapper believed her abduction to be a mistake. If so, then maybe going after Joelle had been, too, and it could mean she was no longer in danger. Duncan had to hope for the best and prepare for the worst, though, and that meant making this trip to the sheriff's office as safe as possible for her and their baby.

Thankfully, no one fired at him when he raced outside and to the cruiser, and he moved fast to bring the vehicle closer to Joelle. Duncan lifted his hand in a wait gesture, though, and didn't give her the go-ahead to move until he'd gotten back out of the cruiser first to open the passenger's side door for her and also so he could shield her as best he could.

All of these security measures had to be both a blessing and a curse for her. After all, Joelle was a good cop, as good as they came, and she was normally in the role of the protector. Added to that, it was probably especially uncomfortable for her since he was the one doing the protecting. But like him, she needed to take all available precautions for their child.

The moment Joelle was inside the cruiser, Duncan hurried back to the driver's seat, and he got them out of there fast. Again, though, he had to keep watch since it was possible for a sniper to be perched on top of one of the buildings that lined Main Street. Thankfully, they made it the six blocks without anyone trying for round two of an attack.

Duncan parked right out front, and they both hurried into the building. Which was practically empty. No surprise there since he had the deputies working the crime scenes at Molly's and Joelle's and others out looking for the gunman. The sole occupant was Carmen Gonzales, a reserve deputy who'd retired several years earlier but still made herself available for emergencies. This was definitely an emergency.

"Any word about Molly?" Carmen immediately asked.

"Nothing confirmed, but her kidnapper called and claims he'll release her," Duncan explained, and he tacked on a question of his own to that. "Are there any reports from the deputies in the field?"

Carmen shook her head. "Nothing that I didn't forward to Luca and you." She glanced down at the laptop she'd been using when Joelle and he had come in. "I'm doing the background checks on Kate Moreland, her son and his ex-wife, Shanda."

"Good. Keep on that," Duncan instructed, though he wanted to do some digging in those areas as well. "Do you have the son's contact info?"

Carmen checked the computer screen again and nodded. "I'll forward it to you. The phone number for his ex as well."

Duncan muttered a thanks and put his hand on the small of Joelle's back to get her moving first toward her desk in the bullpen where he grabbed her laptop. Then, he picked up his from his office before heading to the break room at the back of the building.

"The doctor said you should rest," he reminded her.

"I can rest and work at the same time," she was quick to respond.

Duncan had expected that and already come up with a compromise. He took her to the break room with him where there was a fairly comfortable sofa, had her sit and then handed over the laptop.

"I want you to contact the techs at the crime lab and see if they can get anything from the number Molly's kidnapper used to call us," Duncan instructed. "That's priority."

Even though both of them knew that was a long shot. The kidnapper had probably used a burner that couldn't be traced. Still, they might get lucky.

"After that, if you're not ready to get some actual sleep, I need any and all preliminary reports from the CSIs and fire department," he continued.

"I won't be ready to sleep," she assured him. "Not with the adrenaline still burning through me."

Yeah, he knew all about adrenaline overload. Hard to come down from that, and when you did, it was a crash.

Joelle would no doubt soon be exhausted. Maybe enough that she'd actually grab a nap.

He went to the small fridge in the corner and took out two bottles of water and one of Joelle's yogurt cups she kept stocked. He set one of the waters, the yogurt and a spoon on the end table next to her.

"Also, if you still have any bandwidth left after dealing with the techs and getting the reports, go through the file of Shanda's arrest. See if there are any red flags that could have predicted something like this."

It wasn't busy work, and Joelle knew that because she got started on it right away. All were necessary steps in the investigation. So was what Duncan had to do next. Despite the fact it was barely five in the morning, he used the contact info Carmen had just emailed him and called Brad Moreland. There was no answer for four rings, and just as Duncan thought the call might go to voice mail, someone finally answered.

"What?" a man snarled, and judging from the grogginess in his voice, Duncan had woken him up.

"I'm Sheriff Duncan Holder from Saddle Ridge. FYI, this call is on speaker, and I have a deputy listening. Are you Brad Moreland?"

The man cursed. "Saddle Ridge," he spat out like venom. "Yeah, this is Brad Moreland, and anything you want to say to me should go through my lawyer. We're going through with the lawsuit for what you did to my wife."

"Your ex-wife," Duncan corrected. "And what lawsuit?" He figured he'd get that out of the way before bringing up the reason for this call.

"My wife," Brad snapped. "Shanda and I are reconciling. And as for the lawsuit, you'll soon know all about that because we're filing a civil suit for my wife's unlawful arrest and detainment. An arrest and detainment that was so traumatic she ended up miscarrying."

Bingo. There it was. The motive all spelled out. Though it did seem odd that they'd file a civil suit, which would draw attention to themselves. That could mean they weren't behind the attack and Molly's kidnapping. Or else they wanted to use the civil suit as a sort of reverse psychology. Why go after them physically when they were already going the legal route?

"We're going to sue you and your department into the ground," Brad threatened. "And then we'll go after your personal assets. You and your deputies aren't above the law, Sheriff." Again, he used that venomous tone for the last word.

Since Shanda's arrest had been justified, Duncan seriously doubted there'd be a payout of any kind, but a civil suit was an annoyance since he would still have to defend the actions the former sheriff had taken. That would in turn stir up bad memories for Joelle.

One look at her face confirmed it was already doing that.

"You and the deputies are going to pay for—"

"I'm calling about your mother, Kate Moreland," Duncan interrupted.

Brad clearly hadn't expected him to say that because it stopped his tirade, and after a few seconds of silence, the man muttered, "What about her?" There was concern, but then the anger returned. "Did you come up with some reason to arrest her?"

"No." Duncan took a moment to consider what he intended, and didn't intend, to say. "She was involved in a car accident and was taken to the hospital."

Brad cursed. "Is she alive?"

"She is." And he waited to see how Brad would react to

that. If Brad did, indeed, have criminal intentions as his mother claimed, then the man might have wanted the news that the car crash had been fatal.

"I need to see her," Brad insisted. "Where is she?"

"She's in the hospital and in protective custody."

There was some more cursing. "*Your* protective custody. This from the sheriff's office that killed my child and wrecked my life—"

"It's odd that you'd mention someone being killed because that's what your mother claimed you wanted to do."

That brought on the silence. "You're lying."

"I have witnesses," Duncan pointed out.

Brad huffed. "Witnesses who you coached no doubt because you want to get ahead of the lawsuit and try to defame me."

"I didn't know about the lawsuit before I called you. Now, explain why your mother would accuse you of plotting to kill a cop." Duncan made sure that wasn't a suggestion but rather an order from a sheriff.

"I have no idea." Now there was plenty of defensiveness in Brad's voice. "You said she was in a car accident so maybe she got a head injury and was confused."

Duncan hadn't missed the fact that Brad hadn't asked about his mother's injuries right from the start. Most people did once they understood their loved one was alive. Brad had demanded to see her, but he hadn't pressed about her condition.

"Is my mother in the hospital there in Saddle Ridge?" Brad finally said after a long silence. "If so, I can be there in under an hour."

"She can't have visitors. Doctor's orders. But even if she could, I won't let you in to see her unless I'm convinced your mother was wrong about you wanting to kill one of my deputies."

"Deputy Joelle McCullough." Brad said her name like profanity. "She was one of the cops who arrested my wife. Oh, her dad was the head honcho in that, but he's dead so the lawsuit will be aimed mainly at his daughter and the other cops involved. Molly Radel and Ronnie Bishop."

Everything inside Duncan went on alert, and he mouthed for Joelle to send Ronnie a heads-up about being a possible target.

"It's interesting that out of the three people you just named," Duncan continued with Brad, "one was kidnapped and the other attacked. According to your mom, she specifically came to Saddle Ridge to warn Deputy McCullough."

Brad's next round of profanity was quick and raw. "Like I said, my mother was mistaken. Sure, I've talked about Deputy McCullough and Deputy Radel but I'll go after them in the courts for what they did. I'm not on some vendetta."

"So, you have an alibi for the past five hours?" Duncan fired back.

"I was in bed at my house. Alone," Brad tacked onto that in a mutter. "That doesn't mean I did those things."

Maybe. But it didn't look good, not with his mother accusing him and with no alibi. "I want you here at the Saddle Ridge Sheriff's Office in three hours. That'll give you time to arrange for your lawyer to come with you."

"You better believe I'll have a lawyer. And I'll expect to see my mother when I'm there."

"You can expect it, but you might not get it," Duncan snarled right back. "Be here in three hours," he repeated, and he ended the call.

Duncan immediately fixed his gaze on Joelle, prompting her to give her take on the phone call.

"Brad's angry enough to come after Molly and me. And he has plenty of money to hire someone to orchestrate the attacks," she amended and then paused. "But if he hired that gunman and the kidnapper, then why didn't he establish an alibi for himself?"

Yeah, that was the thing that stood out for Duncan, too. "Maybe Brad didn't know his mom was going to rat him out. He also might not have thought we'd connect the kidnapping and attack to what happened to his ex-wife nearly two years ago."

Still, a guilty person should have thought of those angles and covered his butt. Brad hadn't. Was that cockiness, sloppy work or was he actually innocent?

Joelle's phone dinged with a text, and she sighed when she read it. "While you were talking to Brad, I texted the tech guys with the kidnapper's phone number. They obviously took me at my word when I said it was high priority because they checked it right away. It's a burner, and it's no longer in service."

Duncan went with a sigh of his own, even though it was expected news.

"Of course, the tech guys will keep searching to see if they can link it back to anyone," she added.

That was standard operating procedure, but it was a rarity when they found those links. Still, it was all they had at the moment.

"I'm hoping the kidnapper will arrange for us to pick up Molly before Brad comes in for his interview," Duncan said, and he checked the time. "Why don't you try to get some rest—" He stopped when his phone rang. Unknown caller. And his heart raced at the possibility of this being the kidnapper who was using a different phone.

"Sheriff Holder," Duncan answered. He hit record and put the call on speaker. But it wasn't a man's voice who greeted him.

"Sheriff," a woman said. It definitely wasn't Molly, either. "I'm Shanda Cantrell. I just got off the phone with Brad, and he was very upset."

Duncan would have preferred for this call to be about Molly and her release, but he'd intended to call Shanda so this saved him the step of having to get her number.

"A lot of people are upset right now," Duncan verified. "And by the way, I have you on speaker, and one of my deputies is listening. I'm also recording this conversation."

That brought on a couple of moments of silence. "All right," Shanda finally said. "I'm calling because Brad told me his mother was delusional and talking out of her head," Shanda went on. "Kate accused Brad of intending to commit a crime."

"Did he?" Duncan asked, figuring that was the fastest way to cut to the heart of this conversation.

Shanda didn't gasp or make a sharp sound of surprise. Instead, she sighed. "No. Not that I know of," she tacked onto that.

Interesting. Those weren't the words of a woman jumping to defend her ex-husband. "But it's possible he committed a crime," Duncan pressed.

"Not that I know of," she repeated, and this time there was an admonishment to her tone. "I can tell you that the relationship between Kate and Brad is strained right now, so if Kate sustained a head injury or something, that might have caused her to say what she did."

Duncan disregarded the last part of that and went for the meat of the remark. "Strained how? Why?"

Shanda sighed again. "It's because of me. Brad wants to get back together and Kate loathes me."

When Shanda didn't add more, Duncan went with a prompt. "Brad wants to get back together. How about you? How do you feel about that?"

"It's complicated." Shanda groaned. "I know that's a cliché, but in our case, it's true. Brad and I share a very painful past."

Duncan could relate, what with Joelle and him blaming themselves for not stopping her father's murder. So the cliché of complicated fit them, too.

"I'm not sure if Brad and I will be getting back together or not," Shanda finally admitted. "It won't happen unless he's willing to get the counseling he needs. So far, Brad hasn't shown up at any of the appointments I've scheduled for him."

Maybe because the man didn't want to forget the past but rather get revenge for it.

"Counseling has really helped me," Shanda went on. "I had a difficult childhood, and according to my therapist, that created some anger issues. Issues, too, with using people. And, yes, I used Brad. Or rather I used his money. Don't get me wrong. I loved him, and that's why I married him, but I wasn't careful with his money."

Shanda sounded a lot different than she had from the night she'd been arrested. Maybe the counseling had worked. Or maybe this was all an act.

"Why does Kate loathe you?" Duncan asked, circling back to what Shanda had said earlier.

"This is all very personal," Shanda muttered.

"You bet it is," Duncan snarled. "Someone tried to kill

one of my deputies and kidnapped a former deputy who's now a dispatcher. For me, that's as personal as it gets, and if you have any information that can help me find the person responsible, then spill it."

"Yes," the woman said, her voice heavy with emotion now. "Brad told me about that, and he thinks because of what Kate said, he's now a suspect in those crimes."

"He is a suspect," Duncan verified. "And you're a person of interest. In fact, I'll need you to come into the Saddle Ridge Sheriff's Office for an official interview. When we're done talking, go ahead and arrange for that. Bring your lawyer if you want, but I expect you in this morning. The earlier, the better."

"I see," Shanda said in a whisper. "You believe the attack and the kidnapping are connected to what happened to me nearly two years ago."

"Are they?" Duncan was quick to ask.

"No, I don't think so." She paused. "Look, I understand you have a job to do, but that incident was very painful for me. I had a miscarriage, and since I couldn't deal with the grief of losing my child, I fell apart. It ruined my marriage."

Duncan listened for any signs of bitterness and rage, but he didn't pick up on anything. What was there was the pain and grief of trauma. Then again, maybe that's what Shanda wanted him to hear.

"As I said, I've gone through counseling," Shanda went on. "Lots and lots of it. It's helped, but Brad seems stalled in that deep rut of loss over our baby. You see, I'd had a hard time getting pregnant and gone through many fertility treatments. The pregnancy was a miracle, and it was snatched away."

Now there was some bitterness, but Duncan figured it was a drop in the bucket to what Brad had revealed.

"I understand Brad has filed a civil lawsuit over what happened," Shanda went on. "I'm trying to talk him out of that because I don't think that will help with his healing. He needs to heal," she emphasized.

Duncan had to wonder just how "broken" Brad was. Maybe Kate was dead-on when she'd accused her son of going after Joelle.

"Any idea why Brad would wait two years to file the lawsuit?" he pressed.

Shanda sighed. "He's talked about it for a while, months. And I know he interviewed several lawyers before he finally found one who actually encouraged him to go through with it."

So, Brad had shopped around to find someone who had told him what he wanted to hear. And once Brad had that approval, maybe he did more than just start a legal battle. Maybe he decided to get full on revenge.

"Could Brad have been responsible for the attack and kidnapping?" Duncan came out and asked.

"I don't want to believe he is," Shanda admitted. Then, she stopped and muttered something Duncan didn't catch. "I'll contact my lawyer and see if he can meet me right away so we can go to the sheriff's office together. As soon as I have a time for our arrival, I'll let you know."

"I want you in before ten o'clock," Duncan insisted.

"I'll let you know," Shanda repeated, and then she ended the call.

Duncan put his phone away and began to process everything he'd just heard. Judging from the way Joelle's forehead had bunched up, she was doing the same.

"Shanda believes Brad could be guilty," Joelle concluded. "Along with Kate's statement, maybe that's enough for us to get access to Brad's financial records to see if he hired the gunman and the kidnapper?"

"Maybe," Duncan muttered, but he could already hear Brad's lawyer putting up an argument about that. An argument he might win since Kate's own mental state couldn't be verified right now. Still, it was worth a try.

Duncan texted the assistant district attorney to put in the request. He'd have to follow that up with some paperwork, but he might be able to get enough out of Kate and Shanda to justify the warrant.

"You want to try to get some rest now?" Duncan asked her after he'd finished his text.

Joelle opened her mouth, no doubt to argue, but was cut off by the sound of footsteps. Moments later, Carmen appeared in the doorway.

"There's a PI here to see you," Carmen said. "Al Hamlin."

Duncan repeated the name, but it didn't ring any bells. Joelle shook her head to indicate she didn't recognize it, either.

"Did he say what he wants?" Duncan asked.

Carmen nodded. "He claims he knows who kidnapped Molly and tried to kill Joelle. And he says he has proof."

Chapter Five

Joelle slowly got to her feet, her attention fixed on Carmen. She immediately had a bad thought, that this was one of the gunmen using this visit as a ploy to come after Duncan and her again. The concern must have shown on her face, too, because Carmen spoke right up.

"Hamlin didn't set off the metal detector," Carmen pointed out, "but Luca's back, and he frisked him. He was armed with a Glock that he's licensed to carry, but Luca is holding onto that and keeping an eye on him." She shifted her gaze to Duncan. "Do you want to see him, or should Luca interview him?"

"Oh, I want to see him," Duncan assured her. "Take him to interview room one. Joelle and I will be in there in a minute or two."

Carmen nodded, stepped away and then backtracked. "While Luca was frisking him, I ran a quick background on Hamlin. He is a PI from San Antonio but currently living in Austin, and he's twenty-three. That's all I have on him right now, and I'll dig for more, and if anything comes up while you're talking to him, I'll let you know."

"Thanks," Duncan said. "Dig, but finding Molly is the top priority, and I want you to sit on the lab to get the results on the blood that we found at Molly's place. So, don't spend much energy on Hamlin because this visit might turn out to be nothing," he added in a mutter.

Joelle knew Duncan was right about both things. Molly being the priority and this turning out to be nothing. Crackpots surfaced all the time during investigations, and even though there hadn't been that much time between this PI showing up and the attack and Molly's kidnapping, word of it would have already gotten out. Still, Joelle felt herself clinging to the hope that this Allen Hamlin could give Duncan and her some much-needed answers.

"I won't insult you by asking if you're up for doing this interview," Duncan told her once Carmen had left. "But if you want to keep on the searches you're doing, I can handle Hamlin solo."

"I want to hear what he has to say," Joelle was quick to let him know. Oh, yes. That hope was burning bright and hot in her.

Duncan studied her a couple of seconds, not with the heat that was sometimes in his eyes when he looked at her. All right, there was some heat. Always was, but Joelle was certain he was trying to make sure she was holding up okay. She was barely holding on and now battling the dreaded adrenaline crash, but there was no way she would sit this one out.

He finally nodded and tipped his head toward the interview room just down the hall. Judging from the sounds of footsteps and voices, Carmen was already escorting the PI there.

Because Joelle was behind Duncan, she didn't get her first glimpse of Hamlin until they were in the room with him. He looked even younger than twenty-three and was wearing khakis and a white button-down shirt. His short cropped hair was a pale blond. Actually, pale described the rest of him, too, what with his light skin tone and gray eyes. He had a thick envelope tucked under his arm.

"Let me know if you need anything," Carmen muttered to Duncan before she left them.

"Sheriff Holder," the man immediately said, and he extended his hand for Duncan to shake. Duncan did, but before Hamlin had released his grip, he looked at Joelle. "Deputy McCullough. I'm Al Hamlin."

Joelle was a little uneasy that Hamlin could identify them when she was reasonably sure she'd never seen him before. "Have we met?" Joelle came out and asked.

Hamlin shook his head. "I followed news of your father's murder so that's how I knew who you were. Both of you and the other deputies were mentioned in the press a lot."

Father's murder. No way for her not to react to that, but Joelle tried to mask the quick punch of grief. But Hamlin was right about the press. No one in her family or the sheriff's office had escaped the publicity.

"Thanks for seeing me so early," Hamlin said, glancing at both Duncan and Joelle. "You're going to want to hear what I have to say."

Duncan motioned for Hamlin to take a seat, and when he did, Duncan and she sat across from him. "You told my deputy that you had information about two crimes that were committed a few hours ago."

"I do." Hamlin handed Duncan the envelope. "There's a lot of information in there so I'll try to summarize and hit the high points. Five months ago when Sheriff McCullough was murdered, he was investigating a missing pregnant teenager."

"Mandy Vernon," Duncan automatically supplied while he opened the envelope. He took out what appeared to be police reports.

"Yes," Hamlin agreed. "Some thought Mandy had just run away because she wasn't getting along with her folks or her boyfriend, but Sheriff McCullough thought she might have been kidnapped or lured into the hands of someone who wanted her for the baby she was carrying."

Joelle knew that was also true. Her father had been insistent that something bad had happened to Mandy.

"I believe Sheriff McCullough was right," Hamlin went on, and then he stopped and took a long breath as if steeling himself up. "A month ago, my own sister, Isla, went missing. She's seventeen and was seven months pregnant at the time she disappeared. I swear on my life that Isla wouldn't have just left. Like Mandy, I believe someone took her for the baby."

Joelle glanced at the reports again. "Do you have proof?"

"Circumstantial but yes, there's proof," Hamlin insisted. "Over the past year, eight pregnant teenage girls have gone missing in the state, and none has been seen or heard from since." He leaned in, putting his arms on the table, and he looked straight at Joelle. "I believe there's a black market baby ring operating, and that your father found something that could have gotten him killed."

This wasn't a total news flash. Joelle, Duncan and everyone in law enforcement in Saddle Ridge had looked at that connection since it was a case that had occupied a lot of her father's time. But if her dad had actually found anything big related to the investigation, he hadn't put it in his reports. Nor had he mentioned it to anyone. Since three of his kids were cops, Joelle thought he would have told them.

If he'd gotten the chance, that is.

It was possible he'd been murdered before he could reveal something he'd learned.

"Bottom-line this," Duncan said, holding up the one-inch

thick stack of papers he'd taken from the envelope. "Is there proof of any kind for who killed Sheriff McCullough? And for the attack on Deputy McCullough and the kidnapping of the dispatcher?"

Joelle expected the PI to hedge and repeat his *circumstantial*. But he didn't.

"Yes," Hamlin stated, and he gathered his breath again. "Since Isla went missing, I've been digging, and talking to every informant I could. One name kept popping up when people would whisper about a black market baby ring." He paused a heartbeat. "Kate Moreland."

Of all the names Joelle had thought he might say, that wasn't one of them. "Kate?" she questioned.

Hamlin gave a firm nod. "Don't ask me how I got access to her financial records, but something doesn't add up. The woman's bringing in a lot more money than her businesses."

Joelle scowled, and she was certain Duncan was doing the same. "I will ask how you got her financials," Duncan stated, "because if you obtained them illegally, then you don't have proof."

The PI muttered some profanity and shook his head. "The proof is there for someone who can get it through legal channels. I took some shortcuts because I wanted to see if there were any red flags, if this woman could possibly be the person responsible for the disappearance of my sister and other teenage girls. I believe she is," he added with what sounded to be absolute certainty.

"Spell it out for me," Duncan ordered.

Joelle figured Duncan wasn't forgetting about those short cuts that Hamlin had admitted to taking. He'd no doubt get back to those, but if Kate did have some part in Molly's kidnapping, then that was the priority here.

"I have a statement from two women who say that Kate Moreland brokered the sale of their babies," Hamlin went on.

"Their names and details are in here?" Duncan asked, motioning toward the papers again.

"They are." Now Hamlin paused, and some of his enthusiasm waned. "But those incidents happened over ten years ago. There are some more recent," he was quick to add. "However, those women wouldn't go on record."

Playing devil's advocate, Joelle tried to see how this all might have played out. "Isn't it possible that Kate didn't broker the sale of the babies but rather just put the teenagers in contact with prospective adoptive parents?"

Though, so far, Joelle hadn't come across any reference to Kate having done that sort of thing. Still, info like that didn't usually turn up in background checks unless there had been something illegal about it.

"Kate might try to say that," Hamlin answered, "but she'd be lying. The girls said Kate paid them five thousand for the babies."

"Is there any kind of concrete proof of that?" Duncan asked.

"The statements from the girls." Hamlin's voice turned hard, and he huffed. "I figure Kate's been doing this for years, and that she then sells the babies for a whole lot more than five grand." He paused, looked Joelle straight in the eyes. "I also believe when she couldn't find a readily available teenager to give up their kid, then Kate had pregnant adults kidnapped. And I think that's what your father uncovered."

Part of Joelle wanted to latch on to this since it would be a lead not only in Molly's kidnapping but also her father's murder. But as working theories went, it wasn't nearly as strong as Brad's and maybe Shanda's motive. Or what had happened to her father. Because maybe Brad or Shanda had had her dad killed because of the arrest and miscarriage.

Maybe Kate had the same motive as her son.

But then why would the woman have shown up proclaiming Brad was behind the attacks? That didn't make sense, unless...

Joelle's mind followed that through. If Kate was, indeed, guilty of everything that Hamlin was saying, she might want to set up her son to take the blame. But certainly, there'd be someone else, someone not in the woman's gene pool, to try to frame.

"Read the files," Hamlin said after another huff. "You'll see the connections, and you'll see that Kate is guilty."

Duncan made a sound that could have meant anything. He certainly didn't jump on the "Kate did this" bandwagon.

"I'll definitely read through all of this," Duncan assured him, "and I'll want to talk to the two women who gave you their statements about selling their babies to Kate."

Duncan stood, signaling an end to the meeting, and Hamlin clearly didn't approve of what he obviously thought was a brush-off.

"Kate did this," Hamlin snarled. His gaze fired to Joelle. "Arrest her if you want your father's killer behind bars."

"If Kate did it, trust me, she'll be arrested," Joelle confirmed.

That brought on another huff from Hamlin, and he stood and stormed out. They followed him to make sure he did leave the building. After all, everything Hamlin had just told them could have been done to get closer to them, to get them to let down their guard.

Because Hamlin could be one of the gunmen who'd attacked her earlier.

They went into the bullpen, and Hamlin didn't linger. He went straight past Carmen and Luca and out the door.

"Did he actually have proof of anything?" Luca immediately wanted to know.

Duncan lifted the papers. "To be determined. Until we know for sure, though, call the deputy who's guarding Kate Moreland and tell him or her to keep a very close eye on the woman. I doubt Kate's in any shape to leave, but I want to make sure she stays put." His gaze slid to Hamlin who was now on the sidewalk. "And tell the deputy to make sure that guy doesn't get into her room."

Luca glanced at Hamlin, too, and took out his phone to make the call.

Duncan shifted his attention to Carmen. "Get me anything you can find on Hamlin and Kate Moreland. Use the techs to help with that, but I need thorough background checks on both of them."

Carmen nodded and hurried back to her desk.

Joelle looked at the papers. "I can start going through those."

Duncan hesitated, and she knew why. There was probably a lot in there about her father's murder. A lot that would take jabs at some still raw, painful memories.

"It needs to be done," was all Joelle said, and Duncan handed over half the papers to her. He'd almost certainly be poring through the other half.

They went back to the break room but had barely made it inside when Joelle's phone rang. Her heart jolted when she saw *Unknown Caller* on the screen, and she nearly dropped the papers when she fumbled to answer it.

"Joelle," a woman said.

Molly.

Joelle fumbled the papers again to put the call on speaker. "Molly."

Since her voice had way too much breath and hardly any sound, Joelle repeated the woman's name. Duncan sprang into action, taking out his phone and contacting tech so they could try and trace the call.

"Are you okay?" Joelle asked Molly. "Where are you?"

Molly didn't answer right away, but Joelle could hear someone muttering in the background. Even though she couldn't make out the words, she guessed it was the kidnapper giving Molly instructions about what not to say.

"I'm not hurt," Molly finally answered. "And the baby's moving and kicking so I think she's fine, too."

Joelle had so many things she wanted to ask, but she blurted out the first thing that popped into her head. "There was blood at your house."

"It's not mine," Molly said, but then stopped when there was more muttering in the background.

Duncan's gaze flashed to Joelle, and then he fired off a text. And she knew why. If the blood wasn't Molly's, then it likely belonged to the kidnapper, and they could use it to identify him.

"I'm to tell you that he's releasing me in a couple of hours," Molly went on several moments later. "But you're to send him ten thousand dollars to this account." She read off a series of numbers, and Duncan typed them into the notes on his phone. "You can get the money from my savings. I have an inheritance from my grandmother, and once the money's in the account, he'll call you with the location where he's dropping me off."

Ten thousand. That wasn't a huge ransom so maybe the kidnapper just wanted some cash to get away. Joelle was betting that the account would be offshore and not traceable. But they still had the blood.

"He also said I was to tell you not to look for him," Molly added. "Please don't look for him," she said, her voice breaking into a sob. "I just need this to be over, and it won't be if he gets spooked. I need to come home."

"We'll get you home," Duncan promised, but he was talking to the air because the call had already ended.

Duncan took her phone and immediately tried to call Molly back. There was no answer, and Joelle suspected in a minute or two the burner phone would be disabled.

A flood of emotions slammed through Joelle. The relief, the fear, all mixed together with the adrenaline crash. It was a bad combination because she started to shake. She headed toward the sofa so she could drop down onto it, but Duncan pulled her into his arms.

"We will get her home," he repeated, and he eased her even closer to him. Until they were right against each other.

Joelle knew she should move away. But she couldn't. She needed this. Needed Duncan. Even though there'd be a high price to pay for it. This kind of closeness could lead to dangerous feelings. Ones that would drown her in guilt because Duncan was the ultimate reminder that she hadn't saved her father. That she might have been able to stop him from dying or her mother from vanishing if she hadn't been with Duncan.

"I'm okay," she managed to say.

It wasn't anywhere close to the truth, but when the heat came, swirling in with the other emotions, Joelle forced herself to move. Not far. Just one step back, and she made the mistake of looking up and into Duncan's eyes.

Yes, the heat was there. But there was so much more. He was worried about her. Heck, she was worried about herself, about what the stress of this was doing to their baby. The best way to minimize that worry, though, was to try and forget the heat and focus on getting Molly safely home.

"I can transfer the money into that account," she said. Her voice was still shaky. So was the rest of her, but Duncan must have realized, too, that the work was what they both needed now. "I can get it from my savings so we don't have to go through the bank to get it from Molly's."

"Use the sheriff's office funds and instruct the bank to delay releasing the money," Duncan told her. "The kidnapper will see the funds deposited and maybe go ahead and release Molly. Once we have her, we can try to trace the kidnapper's location when he or she attempts to withdraw or transfer the money."

Like her, he didn't seem hopeful of that happening, but they had to check and double check. Even if Molly was safely returned, a serious crime had been committed. The kidnapper, and anyone who hired him, should pay and pay hard.

Since Joelle had never done a transfer like this, it took her several minutes to work through the process of it. While she did that, Duncan called the tech who'd been trying to trace the call. They were both still busy with their tasks when Carmen appeared in the door. She had her laptop balanced in the crook of her arm and continued to read whatever was on the screen until Joelle and Duncan finished.

"The kidnapper was using another burner," Duncan said. "Couldn't be traced, and like the other, it's already been disconnected." He glanced at Joelle. "Did the transfer go through?"

Joelle nodded, and she looked at Carmen. "The kidnapper called again and had Molly tell us that he wanted ten grand."

"Is Molly okay?" Carmen immediately asked.

"She said she was," Joelle relayed. "I hope that's true."

"So do I," the other deputy muttered, and she turned her attention back to her laptop.

"Please tell me you have something on the blood that was found at Molly's," Duncan said to Carmen.

"No. Luca's calling about that now. But I got a preliminary report on Hamlin. Since his sister went missing, he's focused only on that. No other clients."

Duncan huffed and put his hands on his hips. "It's hard to earn an income when you don't have clients."

"He inherited life insurance money from his parents who died in a car accident three years ago. It was about half a million, so I'm guessing he lives off that and apparently devotes all his time to finding his sister. There's no sign of her, by the way," Carmen added. "But Austin PD believes she ran away with her then boyfriend since he went missing, too."

"Is there anything in that prelim report to indicate that Hamlin could have been behind the kidnapping and attack on Joelle?" Duncan asked.

"No criminal record or anything like that, but I'll keep digging. I should be able to get access to the background that would have been done on him to get his PI license. That would give us a bigger picture of him."

"Do that," Duncan said just as his phone rang.

Joelle immediately got to her feet, and everything inside her went tight again until she remembered the kidnapper would likely be calling her number, not Duncan's.

"It's Dr. Benton," Duncan relayed, answering the call. "I'm putting you on speaker so my deputies can hear. I hope you're about to tell me we have the green light to question Kate."

"Not yet. She's sedated, and I want her to stay that way for at least another hour or two," the doctor explained. "I'm calling because I got back her tox results, and I thought you'd want to know."

"I do," Duncan verified. "She was drugged?"

"There were traces of a prescription sleep aid in her system. Doxepin. Traces," the doctor emphasized. "There certainly wasn't enough of it to cause unconsciousness."

Joelle frowned, and she waited for Duncan to ask the question she knew had to be on his mind. "Do you think she faked her symptoms?"

"Hard to say, but it's possible she had some kind of allergic reaction. I'll be checking for that. When I checked her online medical records, there weren't any allergies listed. Not only that, she's been prescribed this particular sleep aid for years. Still, it's possible the drug in combination with something else caused the disorientation and the unconsciousness. As I mentioned earlier, that *something else* could have caused the car accident."

Yes, that could explain it. Joelle recalled seeing the cut on the woman's head.

"How serious is that injury to the head?" Duncan wanted to know.

"We ran a CT scan, and there was no obvious signs of brain damage or even a concussion," Dr. Benton was quick to say. "Once the patient is out of sedation for her blood pressure, I'll do some neuropsychological evals since a CT scan doesn't always confirm a concussion. It's possible, too, that the trauma of the car accident is playing into her reactions."

Duncan's expression let Joelle know he was skeptical about that. But why would Kate have pretended to be drugged? The woman had literally staggered onto Molly's property and then collapsed. Why do that?

Unfortunately, Joelle immediately came up with an answer. A bad one. If Hamlin was right about Kate being a criminal, then maybe her behavior was meant to make her look innocent while also pointing the blame at Brad. But Kate could have also done this to get closer to them. So she could try to do to Joelle what was done to Molly. Still, that seemed an extreme ploy especially since the woman hadn't been on their radar before she'd shown up at Joelle's.

"I still want to talk to Kate once she's awake," Duncan stressed. "I'll also want the results of those tests you mentioned."

"Is she a suspect in the attacks?" the doctor asked.

"A person of interest, but some information has come to light that I need to question her about. It could be related to the murder of Sheriff McCullough."

"I see," the doctor muttered after a long pause. "I'll let you know the moment you can talk to her," he assured Duncan.

When the call ended, Duncan stared at his phone for a moment before his gaze shifted to Joelle. "We really need to dig into Kate's background."

She couldn't agree more. "I'll do that and check for any updates from the CSIs, techs and lab." They had a lot of cogs going in this particular investigative wheel, and any one of them could provide them with answers.

Maybe, *finally*, answers about her father.

Joelle couldn't fully process that. Couldn't deal with the emotions that would bring. She had to rely on the work not only bringing a closure to the case but to help her find the mental healing that had so far eluded her.

Of course, the healing would only be partial. She would still need to know what had happened to her mother.

"I'll get that PI background report on Hamlin," Carmen said, and she headed back toward the bullpen.

Joelle forced her hands to steady on the laptop keyboard while she checked for those updates. There was one which had come a little too late to say that the blood at Molly's hadn't been hers. That comparison had been fairly simple because her DNA was on file. Now that Molly had been ruled out, the sample would have to make its way through the database to see if there was a match.

Since Duncan was already at work on his laptop. Joelle didn't relay the blood news. She just moved on to the next task—finding out if Kate Moreland had something to hide. The basics about the woman meshed with what they had already learned. She owned a lot of businesses she had inherited from her father who'd died a decade earlier.

Joelle continued looking into the woman's personal life. Divorced, ex-husband deceased and only one child. Brad. There were plenty of social media posts about Kate's fundraisers, parties and such, but there were no recent mentions about Brad. Joelle had to go back five months to find them, and she immediately saw a pattern. Before five months ago, Kate had posted many photos of her and her son together. Then, nothing.

Joelle had to wonder about the timing since her father had been murdered five months ago.

From across the room, Duncan's phone rang, immediately getting her attention since it could be news about Molly. "It's Ruston," he said.

She automatically sighed. Her brother was no doubt checking on her again and probably thought she'd try to gloss over how she was doing. Which she would have done. No way did she want her brothers worrying about her any more than they already were.

"Ruston," Duncan greeted, and unlike the other calls he'd been getting, he didn't put this one on speaker.

Joelle couldn't hear what her brother said, but whatever it was had Duncan slowly getting to his feet. "Hell," he spat out.

That caused Joelle to stand as well, and she went to Duncan. "What's wrong? What happened?" And too many worst-case scenarios started flying through her head.

Duncan lifted his finger in a "wait a second" gesture. "You're sure it's her?" Duncan asked Ruston.

The answer he got caused Duncan to curse again, and then he added, "Yeah, call me the moment you know anything." He pressed end call, and he looked at her.

"Is it Molly?" she managed to ask, even though Joelle's throat had seemingly clamped shut.

Duncan shook his head. "It's Shanda Cantrell. She's been murdered."

Chapter Six

Duncan drank more coffee and paced with his phone anchored between his shoulder and ear while he waited for Joelle's brother, Detective Ruston McCullough, to take him off hold and give him the update on Shanda's murder.

It'd been over an hour since Ruston's initial call to deliver the shocking news that Shanda had been found dead just outside her house in San Antonio, and Ruston had only been able to provide the basics. Apparently, Shanda's lawyer had found her dead when he'd gone to her place. Cause of death had likely been a gunshot wound to the chest.

"Sorry about the wait," Ruston said when he came back on the line. "I just got another call from the CSIs out at Shanda's house, and I wanted to hear what they had to say so I could pass it along to you. And Joelle. She's there, right?"

"I am," Joelle verified. She looked too exhausted to pace, the way Duncan was in an effort to burn up some of this adrenaline and nerves. She was on the sofa, watching and waiting.

"How are you holding up?" Ruston asked, and Duncan knew that question was for Joelle.

"We need answers," she replied, clearly dodging her brother's question.

Ruston sighed because that dodge had given him the

answer. His sister was exhausted and worried about everything that had gone on not just since the attack but the events of the last five months. All of this could be linked, and that was a connection that wasn't going to allow Joelle, or the rest of them, to get much rest anytime soon.

"All right," Ruston continued, "here's what I have. At approximately 6:45 this morning, Shanda's lawyer, Frank Salvetti, arrived at her residence in San Antonio. She had called him about a half hour before that and instructed him that she needed him to accompany her to Saddle Ridge right away."

Hell. A lot had gone on in these hours following Joelle's attack. It was barely six in the morning, but it felt as if they'd been at this for days.

"That's a fast, and very early, response for a lawyer," Duncan pointed out.

"Yeah," Ruston agreed. "I'm guessing it's because Shanda either pays him well or else they have a personal relationship that made him react so fast. Not lovers. I've found no proof of that but maybe just friends. Anyway, he found her lying partway inside her door and on her porch, and he called 911. The ME just confirmed that cause of death was the gunshot wound to the chest. No surprise there. I was one of the first on scene, and it was obvious that she'd been shot and bled out."

"Any witnesses?" Joelle asked.

"None, and there were no security cameras. But it's definitely not suicide. No other weapons around, and even though I don't have the report back on it yet, it'll turn out that she was shot at point-blank range. What it looked like to me was that she opened her door to someone, maybe thinking it was her lawyer or possibly because she knew the person, and then she was shot."

Duncan groaned. Ruston was a good cop so his account

was almost certainly what had happened. But with no witnesses and Shanda dead, they didn't have an ID on the shooter.

"Shanda called me about an hour before she was killed," Duncan explained. "I was going to question her about the attack on Joelle and Molly's kidnapping."

Ruston made a sound of acknowledgment. "Joelle had messaged me about that." He paused. "Shanda's arrest could be linked to Dad's murder. Who else knew that?"

"My three suspects," Duncan was quick to say. Technically, he should be using the "persons of interest" label, but in his mind, they were solid suspects. "Shanda's former mother-in-law, Kate Moreland, who's still hospitalized. Shanda's ex-husband, Brad. A hothead who blames your dad, Joelle and a few others for Shanda's miscarriage following her arrest. The third suspect is Al Hamlin, a PI who showed up out of the blue to point the finger at Kate."

Duncan paused to give Ruston some time to consider all of that.

"Who's your top suspect?" Ruston asked several moments later.

"Well, it would have been Shanda before she was murdered," Duncan admitted. "After all, she's the one who lost the baby, and she's got the funds to hire a gunman and a kidnapper." He stopped again, cursed. "And she could have done just that. Hell, maybe one of her hired thugs wasn't pleased with her and killed her. Molly's kidnapper said what he'd done was a mistake so maybe this is the way he dealt with it."

"You have a name for the kidnapper?" Ruston wanted to know.

"Working on it. We collected some of his blood from Molly's house, and it's being processed now."

If the kidnapper had a record, then they might get a quick match. Rarely did he hope someone was a criminal, but in this case, it would make getting the ID much easier.

"Kate Moreland is in the hospital with a deputy guard on her door," Duncan added to Ruston. "I've been trying to call Brad, but he's not answering."

"He's not answering my calls, either," Ruston supplied. "I've sent two uniforms out to his place to check on him. Brad didn't answer the door and didn't appear to be home. Of course, he could be on his way to see his mother before he's due to come in for his interview."

True, and he might not answer his phone if he was on the road. But it occurred to Duncan that Brad could be dead as well, and if so, he wasn't sure how that would have played out. Maybe Kate had gotten fed up with both Shanda and Brad and hired someone to kill them? Or maybe Brad was very much alive and just dodging cops. If so, that moved him to the top spot of suspects.

Duncan heard the sound of approaching footsteps, and he expected to see either Luca or Carmen step into the doorway. But it was Joelle's other brother, Slater, who was the senior deputy in the sheriff's office. He was definitely a welcome sight since there was plenty to do.

Like Ruston, Slater was the spitting image of a younger version of their late father. Tall and lanky with black hair and green eyes. Joelle had gotten the black hair, but she had her mother's misty gray eyes.

"Let me know if you get any updates," Duncan said to Ruston. "I'll do the same for you."

He ended the call and watched as Slater gave both Duncan and his sister long examining looks. Slater sighed because he could no doubt see the exhaustion on Joelle's face.

"I just did a report with the case updates," Joelle said,

maybe to cut off her brother's insistence that she get some rest. "I'll fill in what Ruston just told us and forward copies to you and the other deputies."

Slater didn't address that. He went to Joelle, eased her off the sofa and into his arms. He brushed a kiss on the top of her head and touched his hand to her baby bump. "How's my niece?"

The argument that had been in Joelle's eyes instantly faded, and she returned her brother's hug. "I think she's swimming around in there."

"Good." Slater leaned down and put his mouth to Joelle's stomach. "Hang in there, kid. I just ordered your mom a huge breakfast to be delivered from the diner. Get ready for all kinds of goodies."

"Thank you," Joelle muttered.

Duncan sent him a look of thanks, too, and wished he'd thought of it. Of course, Joelle might not eat. She hadn't touched the yogurt he'd given her earlier, but maybe Slater could give her a brotherly reminder that eating would be good for the baby.

"I managed to postpone my testimony in the trial," Slater explained, going toward Duncan now. "I figured you could use me back here."

"I can," Duncan verified. "We're hoping the kidnapper will be contacting us soon about releasing Molly, and we need a lot of research done on our suspects."

"Brad Moreland, his mother, Al Hamlin," Slater named off. "I saw the report Joelle did about Shanda's murder so she's off the list. As soon as I had Hamlin's name, I contacted a PI friend who lives in San Antonio, and I asked her about him. This particular PI is a *Girl with the Dragon Tattoo* sort of computer whiz, and she's created all these programs to mine data from old internet articles and social media posts." He paused. "And yeah, she sometimes hacks to find what she wants."

Duncan didn't approve of doing something illegal since they wouldn't be able to use the info in court. But at the moment he was for any and everything that helped them solve this so they could get Molly back.

"Did this PI find something?" Duncan prompted.

Slater nodded. "On the drive back here, she called me with what she'd dug up. Six years ago when Hamlin was seventeen, he and his then pregnant girlfriend were accused of trying to extort money from a couple who wanted to adopt the baby. They were convicted as juveniles so that's why the record didn't pop in a normal background check."

Joelle went closer to them. "Of course, Hamlin didn't mention that to us. What happened to the baby?"

"Unknown. The baby's mother, Erica Corley, was only in juvie lockup for two months, and she was released when she was eight months pregnant. She disappeared shortly thereafter, but my PI friend is trying to track her down."

"Good," Duncan muttered. "Because it'd be interesting to find out if Hamlin and she did sell the baby. It also makes me wonder if Hamlin's missing sister left because he was pressuring her to sell the child."

"Since I was wondering the same thing, the PI will be looking into that as well," Slater said. "People put all sorts of stuff on social media so she might be able to find something that'll clue us in to Isla Hamlin's disappearance."

Duncan made a quick sound of agreement just as he heard a shout coming from the bullpen. And the shout came from a voice he instantly recognized from the phone conversation he'd had with him.

"Sheriff Holder?" Brad called out.

So Brad had surfaced after all, and Duncan was a little

surprised that he'd actually come in as scheduled without being further prodded. Surprised and very much interested in what the man had to say. With Slater and Joelle following him, Duncan went into the bullpen to find the sandy-haired man struggling to get past Luca who was trying to frisk him. Carmen had stepped in to help, but Slater moved toward the trio, too.

"Settle down," Slater snapped to Brad. "You don't get past this point until we're sure you're not armed."

"I'm not armed," Brad snarled, and he aimed a venomous glare at Duncan. "Shanda's dead. Dead," he repeated, his voice breaking on the word. "You should have stopped that from happening. You shouldn't have allowed her to die."

Brad's voice didn't just break that time. He began to sob, tears spilling down his face. He also stopped struggling with the search.

"He's not armed," Luca told Duncan. "What do you want me to do with him?"

"Interview room one," Duncan said. Because one way or another, he intended to get answers from Brad.

Since Brad wasn't steady on his feet, Slater took one side of him and Luca took the other. They maneuvered him to the interview room, sat him in the chair, and Joelle got a box of tissues and a bottle of water. What none of them did was give Brad any sympathetic looks because they all knew this could be an act.

That they could be looking at a killer.

"Let me know if you need me," Luca muttered, heading back toward the bullpen.

"Same here," Slater said. "I'll do some more of that digging we were talking about."

That no doubt meant Slater was going to try to find Hamlin's old girlfriend, Erica. Duncan hoped he could manage it since Erica, who'd now be in her mid-twenties might be able to provide them with some insight into Hamlin.

Duncan and Joelle sat across from Brad and didn't say anything for several minutes. They just waited for Brad to cry it out. When he finally reached for a tissue to dry his eyes, that was Duncan's cue to get started. However, Brad beat him to it.

"Who killed Shanda?" Brad asked. The anger was back in his voice now. "Was it my mother?"

Duncan didn't respond to that. Well, not a direct answer, anyway. Instead, he read Brad his rights, and he didn't think it was his imagination that Brad became more incensed with each line of the Miranda warning.

"Do you understand your rights?" Duncan asked when he'd finished.

"Of course, I do," Brad snapped. "You're covering your butt, but there's no need. I didn't kill my wife."

"Do you understand the part about your right to have your lawyer present?"

"I do, and he'll be coming in soon, but I don't want to wait for him to get answers. I need to know now. Did my mother do this?"

"Your mother is under guard at the hospital," Duncan reminded him. Of course, that didn't mean Kate hadn't hired someone to do it. He leaned in and stared at Brad. "Did you kill Shanda?"

Outrage bloomed across his face, and his mouth dropped open. "No, I did not." Brad snapped out each word. "I loved her, and we were getting back together."

"Maybe," Duncan concluded. "I talked to Shanda right before she was killed, and she didn't confirm a reconciliation. Just the opposite."

No trace of Brad's tears remained, and his eyes narrowed. "I don't believe you. You're lying to provoke me."

"I'm repeating to you what she told me."

Duncan withheld anything else about that conversation he'd had with Shanda, and he let the silence roll through the room. In his experience, most people being interrogated or interviewed were uncomfortable enough with the silence that they started talking.

It worked.

"Shanda wanted me to see a shrink," Brad finally admitted. "She wanted me to rehash the past."

"Isn't that what you're doing with the civil suit?" Joelle asked.

Now Brad turned those narrowed eyes on her. "No. That's retribution. That's payment for a wrong that you and your father did." He stopped and visibly reined in some of the anger. "I thought the best way for Shanda and me to move on was to get back together and start that family she's always wanted."

Interesting. Not the family *we'd* always wanted. "You wanted to have a child with Shanda?" Duncan came out and asked.

"Of course." Brad had gone back to snapping. "And now that won't happen because she's dead."

Brad made the sound of a sob, but Duncan saw no fresh tears in his eyes. Being the cynic that he was, Duncan wondered if the man had tapped his supply of fake drama.

"I understand you called Shanda after you and I had our phone conversation," Duncan said, shifting the conversation a little.

Brad nodded, attempted another sob, and he must have given up on that because he pressed a tissue to his eyes. "I told her what was going on, and I said I wanted to see her. She said we could meet for lunch after I was done with my interview." He stopped again. "If I'd gone over to her place then and there, she might not be dead. I could have stopped her from being killed."

Maybe that was true. But not the truth if Brad had been the one who'd pulled the trigger.

"Where were you from the time you got off the phone with me and Shanda's murder?" Duncan pressed.

"Home," Brad was quick to say.

Duncan was just as quick with a response. "Can anyone verify that?"

"I was alone," the man snapped. "But I tried to make some calls to my mother so it's possible those can be pinpointed to my house."

Yeah, it was possible. But it wasn't proof. Someone could have used Brad's phone to make it look as if he were home. And even if Brad had personally made the calls, it didn't mean his hired gun hadn't been doing his bidding. Still…

"I want permission to get access to your phone records," Duncan insisted. "If you don't agree, I'll assume you have something to hide, and I'll get a search warrant."

Brad didn't seem especially bothered by that. "I'll give you permission," he said, making Duncan silently groan. It meant any communication Brad might have had with hired guns had likely been done through a burner. Maybe one like the ones Molly's kidnapper had been using.

Next, Duncan went with an outright lie, something he was allowed during questioning. "We have footage from security cameras up the street from Shanda's. It's being analyzed as we speak, but I already know there was a vehicle in the area. A vehicle matching the description of one registered to you."

Brad sprang to his feet. "It wasn't mine. I wasn't anywhere near Shanda's this morning."

That might be true. Might be. But Brad could have hired someone to kill her. And that led Duncan to motive.

"Here's my theory," Duncan started. "You arranged to have Deputy McCullough killed or kidnapped. Ditto for the dispatcher who was also a deputy during Shanda's arrest two years ago. Shanda either found out what you'd done or you told her, and when she said she was going to the cops, you made sure she wouldn't be talking to anyone."

If looks could have killed, Brad would have finished off Duncan and Joelle on the spot. He sank back down into his chair. "This interview is over," he insisted, taking out his phone. "I'm not saying another word until I have my lawyer here."

Duncan didn't press, and he figured he could use the time before the lawyer arrived to assemble as much of a case as he could against Brad. What he needed was some physical evidence, something that would get him an arrest warrant so he could take Brad off the streets. Of course, if Brad was the killer, it was possible he'd already set hired guns in motion for another attack.

Joelle and Duncan stepped outside the interview room, closing the door behind them, and they looked at each other. "You believe him?" Joelle whispered, taking the question right out of Duncan's mouth.

Duncan had to shrug. Then, he groaned and scrubbed his hand over his face in frustration. "I want to believe he's the killer, but I'm not sure."

Since he didn't want Brad to overhear any part of this conversation, he motioned for Joelle to follow him back to the break room.

"Everything we have on Brad is circumstantial." He took out his phone. "I'll have Carmen get Brad to sign the agreement to get his phone records. If he's still willing to do it, that is. And there might be something in his call history that could help us get a warrant for his financials."

Duncan fired off a quick text to Carmen, but before he got a reply, his phone rang with an incoming call from Dr. Benton. Duncan couldn't answer it fast enough.

"Kate is awake, and she's insisting on seeing Joelle and you," the doctor said without a greeting. "Obviously, I'd like for her to hold off on that for another hour or two, but she got agitated when I suggested it. Can the two of you come to the hospital now?"

"Absolutely," Duncan readily agreed. "We'll be there in about ten minutes."

Joelle and he hurried back to the bullpen, and Duncan saw the instant alarm on the three deputies' faces. "Brad decided to wait for his lawyer," Duncan explained because the deputies had obviously thought Brad had done something to provoke them. "Joelle and I need to get to the hospital to question Kate Moreland."

"I can go with you for backup," Slater immediately volunteered.

Duncan nodded and got them moving toward the door. After he'd checked to make sure there were no threats lurking around, they got into the cruiser with Joelle in the back seat, Duncan in shotgun and Slater behind the wheel.

As expected, it was not a peaceful, relaxing ride. They were all very aware that the hired guns could be nearby, ready and waiting to strike. It was the reason Duncan had considered asking Joelle to stay behind. But not only wouldn't she have agreed to that, Kate had asked specifically to see her. It was possible the woman would say something to Joelle that she wouldn't to Duncan.

When they reach the hospital, Slater parked by the ER doors so that Joelle and he could hurry inside. Slater got out as well, and Duncan knew he would stand guard, watching for any kind of danger. Simply put, if any hired guns came into the hospital after Joelle and him, Slater would be the first line of defense against that.

Also as expected, there was a reserve deputy outside Kate's room. Anita Denny. Since she obviously recognized Duncan and Joelle, she opened the door and motioned them inside.

"She's waiting for you," Anita, the reserve deputy, informed them.

They stepped into the room and saw that Anita was right. Kate was, indeed, sitting up and clearly expecting them. She didn't look drowsy but rather alert and very worried.

"A friend of mine called the hospital and left a message to tell me that Shanda had been murdered," Kate immediately said. "Is it true?"

Later, Duncan would want to know the name of that friend. For now, though, he basically did a death notification.

"I regret to inform you that Shanda was murdered earlier this morning," he told her while he carefully watched her reaction.

A reaction that included widened eyes and a shudder of her breath. Kate touched her fingers to her mouth that trembled. "I'd hoped it wasn't true. I didn't want it to be true," she amended.

Duncan didn't have time to treat this like a normal death notification. He needed to jump right into questions that had to be asked. And he had to start with the basics.

"I'm going to Mirandize you," Duncan stated. "It's to cover the legal bases and make sure you're aware of what your rights are."

Kate didn't ask why he was doing this. She merely sat

and listened while he finished, and then she nodded when he asked if she understood everything he'd just spelled out.

Since Kate didn't voice any kind of objections, Duncan continued, "From what I've heard, Shanda and you didn't have a good relationship. You were at odds. In fact, when I spoke to Shanda before she died, she claimed that you loathed her."

Kate didn't show any flares of temper as Brad had done. The woman sighed and shook her head. "I did loathe her," she admitted. "I thought she didn't handle her miscarriage and divorce nearly as well as she could have, and I believe she never actually loved Brad."

Duncan lifted an eyebrow. "I didn't pick up on that last part from either Brad or Shanda."

"You wouldn't have." Kate glanced away, groaned softly. "Brad was blindly in love with her, and he couldn't see Shanda for what she was. A gold digger. That big house she lives in? That was part of her divorce settlement. She took half of Brad's money when she divorced him."

Now there was some anger, but she kept her gaze pinned downward while she picked at the sheets covering her. Duncan had to wonder if she was looking down so he wouldn't be able to see some truth that she couldn't conceal in her eyes.

Truth that she was glad Shanda was dead. And that she was the one who'd made that happen.

"I should tell you something in case it comes up later," Kate said. "I don't want you to think I'm withholding anything."

"I'm listening," Duncan assured her.

"On the night Shanda was arrested, she and I were arguing on the phone. A very heated argument," Kate emphasized. "I'd called her about some charges I saw on Brad's credit card. Shanda had gone to a high-end boutique and treated herself to the best the place had to offer. I'm talking nearly ten grand. Shanda said that Brad had given her the shopping trip as a surprise gift, and I told her that Brad wasn't paying the bills, that I was." She stopped. "Anyway, Shanda was yelling at me and that's probably why she was driving erratically."

Duncan had known about this. It'd been in the statement Shanda had given. Well, she'd given a thumbnail of it, anyway. She'd told Sheriff McCullough that she'd been having a dispute with her mother-in-law.

"You must have been very upset when you found out that Brad and Shanda were getting back together," Joelle threw out there. All sympathy. Fake, of course. But Duncan knew she was going for the "good cop" angle here. That gave Duncan the leeway to go badass.

"I was," Kate muttered. "I thought it would only lead to Brad being crushed all over again." Now she finally looked up, her attention going to Joelle. "Crushed," she emphasized. "Brad was never the same after the miscarriage and his marriage breaking up."

That was Duncan's cue to jump in. "Is that why you went to Molly's to accuse Brad of trying to kill Joelle?"

On a heavy sigh, Kate closed her eyes. But she nodded. She took in a few shallow breaths, opened her eyes and looked at Joelle again. "I'm sorry, but Brad blamed you and your father for what happened to Shanda. He should have blamed Shanda herself. She's the one who got herself arrested. Instead, Brad decided she wasn't at fault and that the cops involved needed to pay."

"Pay by killing me and kidnapping a former deputy?" Joelle supplied.

Kate nodded again and repeated her apology. "I think

my son has had some kind of mental breakdown. I blame Shanda for that. She led him on, making him believe she'd get back together with him, but there were always new conditions for a reconciliation. One day, she'd say he had to go to counseling. The next, she'd tell him he had to cut me out of his life." She paused. "And he did."

Neither Brad nor Shanda had mentioned that so Duncan had no idea if it was true. However, it was something he would definitely ask Brad about.

"It must have hurt when Brad did that," Joelle murmured.

"It did." There was another flash of anger in her eyes, but Kate seemed to quickly shut that down. "It cut me to the core."

"And that cut made it easier for you to go to Joelle and tell her that Brad wanted her dead," Duncan pointed out.

Kate's mouth tightened for a couple of seconds. "Yes, it did make it easier," she confessed. "If my son hadn't basically disowned me, I might not have been willing to believe the worst about him. But I do believe it. I think Shanda convinced him to go after the people who arrested her. I think this was all her doing."

That was possible, but there was a big question mark in that theory. "Then, why is Shanda dead?"

"Maybe she hired the wrong people to do her bidding, and it backfired." Kate offered that up so quickly that it was obvious she'd given it some thought. "If you play with fire, sometimes you get burned."

"So, you don't think Brad would have killed her?" Joelle asked.

Kate stayed quiet a while. "I don't want to believe he would, but it's possible. Shanda broke him, so anything is possible."

Duncan wasn't sure about the broken part, but it was obvious that Brad had some serious issues. Obvious, too, that he could have certainly murdered his ex-wife.

"I saw your tox results," Duncan said, and he noted the flash of surprise in Kate's eyes. She hadn't been prepared for a quick shift in topics. "There didn't seem to be enough of the sleeping aid in your system for you to behave the way you did when you arrived at Molly's."

Kate stared at him and touched her fingers to the bruise on her forehead. "This must have caused the wooziness," she said. "That and maybe my blood pressure." She paused again. "But I don't recall taking any of my sleeping pills that night. In fact, I'm sure I wouldn't have since I'd planned on driving to Saddle Ridge to see Joelle."

Duncan and Joelle exchanged a glance, and it was Joelle who voiced what they were thinking. "You believe someone might have drugged you with them?"

"Yes," Kate muttered. She squeezed her eyes shut for a moment. "Brad came to see me as I was getting ready to leave. He was furious because I'd shut off his accounts and canceled his credit cards. I was paying him a hefty salary to manage some of my businesses," she added. "I figured since he'd disowned me, then he shouldn't have access to that money." Her mouth tightened again. "He'd planned on buying Shanda another big engagement ring and was enraged when his credit card was declined."

"You two argued?" Duncan prompted when Kate went quiet.

"Yes. A loud ugly argument. I poured myself a shot of scotch, and it's possible Brad could have put one of my sleeping pills in it."

Now Duncan was the one to shake his head. "Why would he have done that?"

"I don't know. To get back at me," Kate suggested. "Maybe

because he realized I was going to see Joelle. I didn't tell him that, but it's possible he guessed since just the day before he'd been ranting about how much Joelle needed to pay for what'd happened to his precious Shanda."

Duncan still wasn't convinced. "If Brad wanted to drug you so you couldn't drive to Saddle Ridge, why not put more than one pill in the drink?"

"Because he might not have wanted to risk me tasting it," Kate answered without hesitation. "And I probably would have. I did notice a funny taste after I drank the scotch in a big gulp, but I didn't think anything about it. Not until later, when I was here at the hospital."

Everything the woman was saying could be true. Or it could all be lies. Duncan knew he was going to have to compare Kate's and Brad's responses side by side and try to figure how this had actually all played out.

Joelle's phone rang, the sound shooting through the silence that had fallen over the room, and he saw *Unknown Caller* when Joelle showed him the screen.

"We have to take this," Joelle said, and Duncan and she went out into the hall. They moved away from Kate's door before Joelle accepted the call.

"Thanks for wiring me the money," the man said. "I'm taking Molly to the drop off now."

It was the kidnapper, the same one who'd called earlier.

"Where?" Joelle asked.

"You'll know soon enough," the man said. "Keep your phone ready because in exactly twenty minutes, I'll be calling you back to come and get Molly."

Chapter Seven

Even though Joelle knew that Duncan still had plenty more questions for Kate, that would have to wait. Twenty minutes wasn't a lot of time to get ready for the kidnapper to drop off Molly.

Or for the kidnapper to put the finishing touches on a ploy to draw Duncan and her out.

Joelle was well aware that might be the case. So was Duncan, and he would almost certainly insist that she stay at the sheriff's office. That wasn't what Joelle wanted to do, but she figured she would end up going along with it. There was no need to put the baby at even greater risk.

"I'll have to come back to finish this interview," Duncan told Kate, and he didn't wait for the woman to respond. He motioned for Joelle to follow him, and they headed out the door.

"Keep a close watch on Kate," Duncan muttered to Anita. "And if she makes any calls, I want to know about it."

Yes, because Kate could be behind whatever was about to happen, and she might want to make a call to someone she'd hired to do her bidding.

They hurried back toward the ER doors where Slater was waiting for them. The moment they were back in the cruiser, Duncan took out his phone. "I need to assemble some backup," he muttered.

Yes, that was a must, and Joelle could see how this could play out. She'd man the sheriff's office, probably along with Luca and Carmen, and then every other available deputy would go with Duncan. Joelle prayed that would be enough protection if something went wrong.

Before Duncan could even make a call, her phone rang, and Joelle frowned when she saw the *Unknown Caller* on the screen. She showed it to Duncan, and the sudden alarm on his face no doubt mirrored hers. Joelle answered, put it on speaker, and the kidnapper's voice poured through the cruiser.

"Molly's at the former sheriff's house," the man snarled.

Oh, mercy. *There.* It would be there. The house where Joelle had been raised. But where her father had also been murdered. She hadn't been able to step inside the place since the initial investigation.

In the background, Joelle heard Molly call out, "Joelle." That was all Molly managed to say before the kidnapper issued an order for her to shut up.

"If you're not here in ten minutes, the deal is off," the man warned them.

"But you said twenty minutes," Duncan snarled right back.

"Ten," the kidnapper repeated.

Slater and Duncan both cursed. "I want proof of life," Duncan demanded.

The kidnapper cursed, too. "You already got it. You heard her yell Joelle's name."

"That could have been a recording," Duncan pointed out.

Joelle hadn't considered that, but it was possible. Likely, even, if the kidnapper had already dropped off Molly some-where else and was putting some distance between him and her. Added to that, Duncan didn't really have any bargaining power since the money had already been transferred. They'd had no choice about that, though, since it had been the kidnapper's only demand for Molly's release. Now these new demands with the quick time restraints spelled trouble.

More cursing from the kidnapper. "Tell him you're alive," the man growled.

Seconds ticked off, and Joelle had to breathe because her lungs were starting to ache. "I'm alive," Molly finally said.

"Where are you?" Duncan asked her.

"I'm not sure. I'm blindfolded, but it's possible I'm at the McCullough ranch like he said."

Possible. But maybe the kidnapper had her elsewhere. Still, Molly was alive, and Joelle was going to latch on to that.

"Don't be late," the kidnapper added. "You wasted one of your minutes with all this yakking. Be here in nine minutes, Sheriff." He ended the call.

"This is a trap," Slater spat out, and his gaze met Joelle's in the rearview mirror.

She couldn't disagree. It had all the markings of a trap, but there was another factor here.

"He has Molly, and we have to get her back," Joelle stated. "The cruiser is bullet-resistant, and I'll stay inside. Yes, this might be a ruse so he can come after me, but he could do that at the sheriff's office, too. In fact, that might be what he has in mind. Get all of you hurrying there to the ranch while he's already right here in town."

Both Slater and Duncan knew that was true, and this was definitely a "damned if you did, dammed if you didn't" situation. Duncan seemed to be having a very short mental debate about that.

"Go to your dad's house fast," Duncan instructed, and like Slater had done to her earlier, he looked at her, the worry in his eyes. "I'm sorry," he muttered.

"Don't be. Let's go get Molly," she said. "Who should I call for backup?"

A muscle flickered in Duncan's jaw when it tightened. "Have dispatch send all available deputies to the location."

Joelle made the call, already calculating how long it would take them to arrive. Too long probably, and the kidnapper would likely know that. Would likely know, too, the emotional punch that her father's house would have for her. She hated these sick mind games. Hated the person who'd set all of it into motion.

She checked the time. They'd already burned one of those nine minutes, and she didn't know the exact time it would take them to get to the ranch. At the speed Slater was going, though, they should make it with maybe a minute or two to spare. A minute or two they wouldn't have had if Duncan had insisted on taking her back to the sheriff's office.

The question was what would they face once they were there at the ranch?

"You want me to call my ranch hands and have them meet us there?" Slater asked Duncan.

"Do that. Have them stay back, though, until they get the word we need them."

He was thinking this could turn into a gunfight. And it possibly could. Joelle tried not to think of the risk this would be to her baby. Especially since Molly and her child were in even greater danger.

While Slater threaded the cruiser around the curvy country roads, Joelle fixed the image of her family's ranch in her head. Of course, she knew every inch of the house and grounds. Knew, too, that there were plenty of places for someone to lie in wait for them. It didn't help, either, that there was no one working full-time at the ranch. Slater often sent over his own hands just to check on the place, but there likely wouldn't have been anyone around when the kidnapper had set all this up. Which could have been hours ago. Heck, he could have been holding Molly here all along, though that would have been risky since eventually, when Duncan had had the manpower, he would have sent someone out to check the place.

"The second floor of the house will be a good place for a sniper," Joelle said. "Not the roof, though, because of the steep pitch."

"There are four front-facing windows on that second floor," Slater added.

Duncan had been to the ranch many times so he no doubt knew all of this, but Joelle thought it wouldn't hurt to spell out the potential points for an attack.

"From the barn loft," she went on, "there's a direct view of the road so anyone there would be able to see the moment we arrive."

Duncan muttered a sound of agreement and took out his gun. "Try to call the kidnapper again and see if he'll give us Molly's exact location. Yeah, it's a long shot," he grumbled.

It was, but Joelle tried anyway. As expected, he didn't answer. It rang out, and she figured he was already in the process of disabling it. Not that they would have the time to trace it. No. This was coming to some kind of showdown fast.

The minutes ticked away but so did the miles as Slater drove toward the ranch. He took the curves at a higher speed than he probably should have, the tires squealing in protest, but her brother kept control of the cruiser and ate up the miles.

Joelle had to force herself to breathe again when the ranch's pastures came into view. She hadn't needed proof that things weren't the same as they had been five months ago, but she got that proof, anyway. There was no livestock in the pastures. None of the beautiful palomino horses her father had loved. Those had already been moved to Slater's ranch.

The sun was fully up now, but the morning mist was still hovering over the pasture grass, giving the place an eerie, otherworldly feel. The mist hung around the house, too, and while it wasn't dense enough to conceal a shooter, she couldn't help but think of the smoke. And the fire that had destroyed her house. It was possible the kidnapper would do that here, too.

Slater cursed again, and Joelle soon saw why. There was a man at the end of the long driveway that led to the house. He was standing next to a black truck.

Hamlin.

"What the hell is he doing here?" Duncan grumbled, taking the question right out of her mouth.

"He's armed," Slater was quick to point out.

Joelle had noticed that as well. Hamlin had a gun in his right hand, and he jerked as if about to aim it at them. He didn't, though. Nor did he relax the grip he had on the weapon.

Her first thought was he was the kidnapper, and this was that showdown they'd expected. But she was betting none of them had expected the man to be out in the open like this.

Slater pulled the cruiser to a jarring stop just a few feet away from Hamlin. "Do you see anyone else?" he asked, his gaze already combing the house and grounds.

Joelle and Duncan were doing the same thing. Looking for hired guns that Hamlin might have brought with him, but there was no one visible in any of the second-floor windows or the barn.

Duncan lowered his window a fraction. "Stay put, Hamlin," he called out when the PI began to walk toward the cruiser. "And drop your weapon."

Hamlin glanced at his gun and scowled. Then, he huffed. "What the hell is this? Did you set me up or something?"

"Drop your weapon," Duncan repeated. His voice had a bite to it, but he added even more with the repeat.

On another huff, Hamlin tossed the gun on the ground and lifted his hands in the air. "I haven't done anything wrong," the PI protested.

"Then, why are you here?" Duncan demanded.

"Because you texted me and asked me to come." Hamlin's response was quick. Maybe rehearsed.

"I didn't text you," Duncan informed him, and Joelle noticed that Duncan was continuing to look for anyone else.

Hamlin shook his head. "But you did. My phone's in my pocket. I can show you."

Duncan didn't take him up on that offer, probably because he knew the text had been sent by someone else to set this all up. But what was *this*? "We're here looking for a kidnapped woman, and the kidnapper gave us this location."

That put some alarm in Hamlin's eyes, but since Joelle was plenty skeptical when it came to the PI, she figured that, too, could have been rehearsed. "I don't know anything about that, and I haven't seen anyone else since I got here."

"He could be telling the truth," Slater whispered. "Brad, Kate or the kidnapper could have arranged for Hamlin to come here to muddy the waters. Of course, if it's Brad or Kate, then it means they know all about Hamlin."

Yes, which would mean they'd know he was investigating the sale of babies. And that he believed Kate was behind that. However, Brad could have arranged this, too, if he wanted the cops looking at someone else other than him for Shanda's murder, the kidnapping and the earlier attack.

"There's only a minute left on the kidnapper's deadline," Joelle reminded them. Though she wasn't sure if that deadline applied any longer since they were, indeed, at the ranch.

Where there was seemingly no sign of Molly.

"Yeah," Duncan muttered, and he seemed to take a breath of relief when there was the sound of sirens in the distance. Backup would be there soon. "Hamlin, get face down on the ground, and don't block the road."

Joelle looked at Duncan, but she already knew what he had in mind. He'd leave backup to deal with Hamlin, and the PI would no doubt be handcuffed so he wouldn't be a threat. Good, because Joelle had the sickening feeling they already had enough threats to deal with.

And priority was finding Molly.

"Find out who's in that cruiser and let them know what's going on," Duncan told her just as his phone dinged with a text. "Never mind. It's Woodrow Leonard and Ronnie Bishop. They were on their way back from your place."

That explained how they'd gotten there so fast. It would have put them miles closer since her house was only an eight-minute or so drive from here. And that was a reminder they were already out of time for finding Molly. Of course, the deadline might not mean anything since it could have simply been part of the ruse to get them here, but Duncan apparently wasn't going to take the risk that those ten minutes had been part of the ploy.

"Joelle, text Woodrow or Ronnie and tell them to cuff Hamlin and take his gun," Duncan instructed. "Tell them to be careful and watch for gunmen. Slater, drive closer to the house."

She typed out the text, but Joelle also continued to glance around at their surroundings. Specifically, looking for any signs they were about to be shot at. But no bullets came.

Not yet, anyway.

Slater went slow, no doubt doing his own checking, and he finally came to a stop in the circular drive in front of the house. He positioned the cruiser close to the porch steps but still had a good view of the barn. Of course, that meant any gunman would have a view of them, too.

"Woodrow and Ronnie will deal with Hamlin," Joelle relayed after she got a response from Ronnie. "They'll cuff Hamlin, put him in the back of the cruiser and drive closer to assist."

"Good," Duncan muttered, and he turned to her. "You're staying put. I'm going inside the house to look around."

Oh, that gave her a nasty jolt of fear. "You're not going in there alone."

Duncan's mouth tightened, and she saw the debate in his eyes. "I want Slater to stay here with you in case you're attacked again."

She shook her head. "You're just as likely to be attacked in the house. Slater can go with you, and I can crawl over the seat and get behind the wheel." Her baby bump wasn't so big, not yet anyway, to prevent her from doing that. "Then, I can move the cruiser if necessary."

Joelle didn't want to think of what might make that necessary, but it would almost certainly mean some kind of attack. Maybe a firebomb to the house. But if that happened, she wouldn't be driving away unless Duncan and Slater were out of harm's way and with her.

The debate in Duncan's eyes continued a moment longer, and when he cursed, she knew he'd made his decision. So did Slater. They both reached for their doors.

"Don't get out of the cruiser," Duncan warned her one last time. He looked as if he wanted to add more, so much more, but thankfully he didn't. Now wasn't the time to bring up anything about "if the worst happens."

"Find Molly," Joelle said as they exited the cruiser.

The moment the doors were shut, she climbed over the seat and got behind the wheel while she continued to keep watch. Behind her, she saw Woodrow and Ronnie's cruiser pull to a stop, and in the distance, she heard yet more sirens. More vehicles, too, and Joelle spotted Slater's ranch hands as they arrived. Good. The more, the better.

But "more" didn't help Slater and Duncan right now.

Joelle quickly lost sight of them after Slater unlocked the front door and they hurried into the house. She could imagine, though, that they would immediately start the room-to-room search. It was a big house, and that meant there were plenty of places to check.

Plenty of places for a killer to hide, too.

Added to that, the house didn't have an open floor plan so Duncan and Slater wouldn't be able to do a quick visual sweep to determine if anyone was there. It'd be a slow process, searching through all eight rooms on the bottom floor before going to the second floor and then likely the attic if there was no sign of Molly before then.

She purposely didn't watch the time because she didn't want to mark off the seconds and minutes of the search for Molly. That wouldn't help her stay focused. Just the opposite. She didn't want to think of the extreme danger Duncan and her brother were in. Molly, too.

The baby stirred, a reminder of why she had to stay safe. It was also a reminder of Duncan. For the past five months, she'd worked so hard to keep her distance from him. Worked hard not to feel anything. Because those kinds of feelings also deepened the guilt and grief. But it was impossible to keep him out of her thoughts when they were thrown together like this. The closeness and the danger were breaking down barriers she'd fought to keep in place.

She forced all of that aside for now and tried to get a glimpse of the upstairs windows, to see if Duncan and Slater had made it to the second floor. It was impossible, though, with the way Slater had parked. The eaves of the porch blocked her view.

Another cruiser pulled in behind the others, and her phone dinged with a text. From Luca. We're coming closer, he messaged.

Hamlin is cuffed in the cruiser. Woodrow, Ronnie and I are going to check the barns and the other outbuildings. David will be here any minute now to help.

Deputy David Morales who normally worked the swing shift. Obviously, he'd been called in, and he would probably have his usual partner with him, Deputy Sonya Grover. Since Sonya and Molly were also friends, the woman would have insisted on coming to help.

All possible help would be needed since in addition to the big barn adjacent to the house, there were two smaller barns farther away and four other smaller outbuildings scattered around the grounds. There was even a fishing cabin on the banks of the creek that snaked through the ranch.

Joelle responded to let Luca know that she understood the plan, and she watched as they sprang into action. Not just the two cruisers but the three ranch hands from Slater's ranch. They didn't park near her, though, but rather between the house and the barn, and soon the deputies and hands began to pour from their vehicles. That didn't make her breathe easier, though.

It just meant a gunman would have more targets.

Her phone dinged again, and the relief washed over her when she saw it was from Duncan.

First and second floors cleared. Molly's not there. Heading into the attic now.

That rid her of any relief she'd just gotten. Yes, Duncan and her brother were still safe, there was no gunfire, but Molly wasn't there. It sickened Joelle to think of where the woman could be. And if she'd been hurt or worse. Now Duncan and Slater would have to basically climb a ladder to get into the attic, and there could be a gunman waiting for them.

She caught some movement from the corner of her eye and turned to the side of the house that was on the opposite side of the barn. Joelle immediately saw the white rectangular spots on the ground. Not the lingering morning mist. These appeared to be sheets of paper.

Joelle didn't want to move too far from the front door in case Slater and Duncan had to come running out, but she backed up the cruiser, keeping close to the porch so she could have a better look. Definitely paper and not some kind of explosives. She inched the cruiser back even farther, and she looked down.

Photos.

Four of them.

And her heart skipped a beat. Because they were pictures of her father. Not crime scene photos, either. These had been taken just as the blood had started to seep out from beneath his fallen lifeless body.

Oh, mercy.

The killer had taken these. And had left them for her to see.

Joelle's gaze immediately fired around. Just as there was a blur of motion. A man came charging at the window of the cruiser. Since he was wearing jeans and a gray work shirt, at first she thought it was one of the ranch hands or a deputy.

It wasn't.

She had a split second to realize this wasn't someone she knew, and she drew her gun. Too late, though. The man had a gun rigged with a silencer, and he immediately jammed it against the window.

And he fired.

The point-blank shot blasted through the cruiser, deafening Joelle and creating a half dollar-sized hole in the bullet resistant glass. The pain shot through her head and quadrupled when he fired another shot. Then, another.

For a horrifying moment, she thought she'd been hit. But no. He wasn't aiming at her. He was tearing the glass apart so he could get to her.

He managed it, too.

She turned her gun toward him, ready to fire, but his fist came through the hole, and he knocked her gun away. In the same motion, he unlocked her door from the inside and opened it, dragging her out of the cruiser.

The pain was still ramming into her head and ears, but Joelle didn't allow that to make her forget her training. She had to protect herself. She had to protect her daughter so she tried to ram the heel of her hand into his throat.

He dodged the blow, and before she could try to deliver another one, he grabbed her hair, dragging her in front of him.

"Stay back or I'll kill her," the man snarled.

That's when she realized Luca, Woodrow and two of the ranch hands had their weapons trained on her attacker. There was no sign of Duncan or Slater, but she figured they were racing out of the attic to the sound of that gunfire. Yes, the gunman had used a silencer, but the shots had still made some sounds that cops would have recognized. Added to that, there'd been the breaking glass. That would have alerted them, too.

"Let her go," Luca demanded.

"Not a chance," her attacker growled, and he began to walk backward with her.

He was pulling her hair hard, causing more pain to shoot through her, but Joelle was gearing up to start fighting him. He stopped her with a single sentence.

"Don't do anything stupid to get your kid hurt," he whispered right against her ear.

She didn't pivot and try to throw the punch she'd been planning. Nor did she attempt a kick. Joelle froze for a moment. Her baby. He was threatening to hurt her baby. And he could do it. That's why he'd said it, and he likely thought it was cause her to give up.

It wouldn't.

No way was she going to let her baby be at the mercy of this SOB. If he managed to get her away from the ranch, then heaven knew where he'd take her. And what he'd do to her and her precious child.

Joelle braced herself and got ready to do what she had to do.

Fight.

Chapter Eight

Everything inside Duncan went cold when he heard the shots. Three of them, one right behind the other.

He forced himself not to think, especially about Joelle and their baby. Duncan just scrambled down the attic ladder and started running. Fast. As if Joelle and the baby's lives depended on it.

Because he had the sickening feeling that it did.

Duncan took the stairs two and three at a time to reach the first floor, and he was about to barrel out the front door when something from the living room window caught his eye.

Joelle.

Hell. She wasn't in the cruiser but on the side of the house, and there was a hulking thug with one hand twisted in her hair and the other holding a gun that was pointed at her head. He was dragging her toward the back of the house. Maybe toward a vehicle he had stashed somewhere on the ranch.

Duncan turned around and headed for the back door, and he cursed when he had to waste precious seconds fumbling to get a deadbolt open. He finally managed it. Finally, got onto the back porch. But he didn't run. In fact, he tried to stay as quiet as possible when he made his way to the side and peered around it.

Duncan silently cursed. Then, he prayed.

The thug had his back to Duncan and was manhandling Joelle. The grip he had on her hair had to be excruciating, but she was alive, and Duncan couldn't see any blood. However, he could see Joelle trying to shift her feet as the would-be kidnapper maneuvered her over some kind of photos on the ground. Later, he'd see what those photos were all about, but for now he had to figure that Joelle was attempting to get into a position so she could fight back.

Duncan had to admire her grit, but this was a situation that could get her killed. Even if that wasn't the thug's intention. The fact he was dragging her somewhere meant he wanted her alive, but he might accidently shoot her if this turned into an outright scuffle.

Still, something had to be done. And it wouldn't be a shot since Duncan didn't have a clean one. The guy was big, at least a head taller than Joelle, but he was well aware of that and was hunkering down enough so that someone wouldn't put a bullet in his brain. Even Duncan couldn't risk shooting him from behind because the shot could go through him and into Joelle.

Duncan glanced over his shoulder when he sensed the movement. Not another thug but rather Slater who was quietly making his way to the end of the porch next to Duncan. Slater didn't curse when he saw what was playing out in the side yard, but Duncan suspected there was plenty of silent profanity going on. Plenty of questions, too. Well, specifically one question.

How the hell had this snake gotten Joelle out of the cruiser?

He suspected that a trio of gunshots in the same exact spot and a hefty sized gun had something to do with that. The cruiser was bullet-resistant, but shots could still get through. Or maybe something had happened to force Joelle out of the cruiser. Later, he'd want the answers to that, but for now he focused on keeping Joelle alive.

Duncan kept his gun aimed and ready, and he watched as the thug continued to drag Joelle. Duncan had to duck back out of sight, though, when he saw the guy turn to look over his shoulder. Thankfully, Slater did the same.

Since Duncan didn't want to risk the thug seeing him, he just stood there and waited. It felt like a couple of lifetimes. Bad ones. Long grueling moments with the stakes as high as they could get.

When the thug finally came into view, Duncan could see that Joelle was still squirming, still trying to fight this snake with her bare hands. The guy turned to take another glance behind him.

And that's when Duncan knew he had to make his move.

It was a risk. Anything he did at this point would be. But he tossed his own gun aside and launched himself off the porch, right onto the guy's back.

Duncan didn't do anything to break his fall. Or the thug's. Duncan didn't care if he broke the SOB's neck. Instead, he focused on knocking away the gun that was pointed at Joelle. That was the danger now. That had to be his priority. That and making sure Joelle didn't get hurt in what was about to happen next.

The thug grunted in pain when Duncan slammed into him and then yelled when Duncan's tackle rammed him onto the ground. Duncan didn't try to break his own fall but rather Joelle's. He hooked his right arm around her, cushioning her as best he could. He wasn't sure if it worked, but she didn't cry out in pain.

He hoped that wasn't because he'd knocked her unconscious.

But he soon felt her move, scrambling away from them. Good. Though Duncan knew Joelle wouldn't be running. She would no doubt be looking for a way to help him win this fight. He didn't especially want her to do that, but this was Joelle, and there'd be no stopping her.

Cursing, the thug used his elbow and jammed it right into Duncan's jaw. He could have sworn he saw stars, but he didn't let the pain faze him. Couldn't. Duncan grabbed the guy by the throat and punched him right in the face. There was a satisfying popping sound, followed by a spray of blood that let Duncan know he'd broken the man's nose.

Duncan didn't stop there. He rammed his fist into his throat, a maneuver he knew would disable him. And it did. Sputtering out a hoarse sound that was akin to a death rattle the SOB dropped back on the ground, clutching his throat and gasping for air.

Slater was suddenly right there, with his gun aimed at the man. Joelle was, too, and Duncan guessed that she'd grabbed the thug's weapon and was now ready to use it on him. Duncan was hoping that wouldn't be necessary.

"It's best if he's alive so we can question him," Duncan managed to say.

It was a reminder that he thought Joelle needed because she had her steely gaze pinned to her attacker, and the look in her eyes told Duncan she was ready to put a bullet in the guy if he tried to attack them again. The man wouldn't be able to do that, though, because he'd need breath to manage it, and it'd be a while before he got that back. Added to that, it'd be suicide for him to try to move with two cops— no, make that five—holding him at gunpoint.

Duncan got to his feet as fast as he could. "Where's Molly?" he demanded. "Point if you can't speak."

The guy kept groaning, kept gasping, but he still somehow managed a defiant look. Added to that, he tried to mutter something, and Duncan thought it was "go to hell, Sheriff."

So, he wasn't going to bend. Not at the moment, anyway.

"Cuff him and get him to jail," Duncan told Woodrow and Ronnie. "Charge him with attempted kidnapping and murder of a police officer. No bail for that." He turned to Luca and the others. "Keep searching for Molly. She might be in the vehicle this SOB used to get here."

With those steps set in motion, Duncan took hold of Joelle's arm. She was trembling, but she wasn't in shock, and other than a few red marks on her temple and neck, she didn't appear to be injured. He sent up a whole load of thanks for that.

"It's not safe for you to be outside," Duncan reminded her. "This guy might not be alone."

She looked at him, their gazes connecting, and it seemed as if she was using him as some kind of anchor. A way to stop herself from falling apart. It was one thing for a cop to be involved in an altercation, but it was much worse when the cop was the target. And there were no doubts about that. Joelle had been the target.

Again.

Joelle managed a nod, and she lowered the thug's gun to the side of her leg. Duncan eased it from her hand and passed it to Luca.

"Bag that," Duncan told him, and he got Joelle moving. First, up onto the porch and then into the house since it had already been searched.

The moment they were inside, he pulled Joelle into his arms. Yeah, it was unprofessional, but he'd been scared out of his mind about her getting hurt, and he needed this. Mercy, he needed it.

She dropped her weight against him, melting into his arms, and she made a hoarse sound. Not a sob. He figured she'd fight tooth and nail to stop any tears. But she couldn't totally stave off the effects of an adrenaline slam like this.

"Are you okay?" he asked. "All right, dumb question. Of course, you're not okay, but were you hurt?"

Joelle dragged in a few quick breaths. "I wasn't hurt. And the baby's fine because she's moving around."

That gave him a punch of relief that was even more powerful than the elbow slam the thug had managed into Duncan's jaw. He'd still need Joelle examined, which would mean checking the baby's heartbeat and such, but they'd come out of this a whole hell of a lot better than he'd imagined when he'd first seen the thug dragging Joelle through the yard.

"He shot out the window of the cruiser at point-blank range," Joelle said, her voice a shaky tangle of breath and nerves. "But he could have shot me. He didn't. He was going to kidnap me."

Yeah. Duncan had already gone there, and the "there" would give him some hellish memories for the rest of his life.

"With him being alive, we might be able to find out if he's a hired gun," Duncan said. "Or learn if he's actually the one who orchestrated these attacks." If so, the man wasn't on their radar. "Did you recognize him?"

Joelle shook her head, the movement causing his mouth to brush across her forehead. And that caused her to look up at him. Their gazes connected again and held firm.

She had to be experiencing a whirl of emotions right now. He certainly was. And Duncan figured those emotions played into him lowering his head and touching his mouth to hers. Just a touch, but it packed another punch.

Man, did it.

The heat would have rolled right through him, and he wanted to take her mouth as he'd done the night they'd landed in bed. And they would both pay dearly for that lapse, too. Joelle and he already had enough regrets, and Duncan didn't want this to be one of them. He figured Joelle felt the same.

But he was wrong.

Joelle came up on her toes and kissed him. Not a touch this time. It was a whole lot more. It was hard, hungry and filled with so many of those emotions. So much heat. She seemed to be using it as an anchor, too. Or maybe something that would help her remember she was alive.

"Thank you," she said when she finally pulled back. "You saved my life. You saved the baby."

In the moment, it felt as if they'd crossed some kind of threshold, that some of the old guilt might be lessening. But Duncan figured this was literally just that—*in the moment*—and that once Joelle leveled out from this attack, then she wouldn't want to be kissing him. Well, she might still want the kiss. Might want *him*. But after a little while, that guilt would hold her back just as it had for the past five months.

Duncan didn't have time to dwell on that. Or on the heat the kiss had notched up. He heard Slater call out his name, and Duncan knew he had to make sure nothing else had gone wrong.

"Wait just inside the door," Duncan told Joelle, and he reached down into his boot and came up with his backup weapon.

Since her gun was still somewhere out in the yard, he wanted her to have a way to protect herself. Of course, he was hoping with all the hopes in the universe that she didn't have to do that. Joelle had already been through way too much.

Duncan opened the back door and stepped onto the porch. He had his own gun ready as well, but he didn't see any immediate signs of danger. However, Slater, Woodrow and Ronnie were hurrying toward an outbuilding that Duncan knew Joelle's father had used to store ATVs and other equipment. At least Duncan thought that's where they were going, but they stopped about six feet in front of the shed.

"Ronnie spotted this," Slater added, reaching down and picking up a piece of green fabric that was almost the same color as the grass.

While Joelle did as he'd asked and remained in the doorway, Duncan went down the steps to have a closer look. He couldn't be sure, but it looked like the torn sleeve of a pajama top. Since Molly had been kidnapped when she likely still would have been in bed, the fabric could belong to her.

Slater went to his knees and began pulling at something. Some kind of flat circular metal cover the size of a tire. It was obviously heavy because Slater was struggling with it, and Ronnie dropped down to help him.

Behind him, Joelle gasped, and Duncan whirled around to make sure no one had come up behind her. She was alone, but she had gone pale, and she pressed her fingers to her trembling mouth.

"It's an old well," she said. "It terrified me when I was a kid, and Dad had that cover put on it to make sure no one fell in. It weighs too much for kids to move it. But…" She stopped, groaned. "But a kidnapper could have done it. Molly could be in there."

Hell. That got Duncan hurrying out into the yard to help them.

"The cover's been moved recently," Slater said, still focusing on the task. "You can tell from the grass around it. But whoever moved it put it back in place."

Duncan growled out another "hell," aloud this time. And he hoped if Molly was in there, she was still alive. By the time Duncan reached them, Slater and Ronnie had already dragged the cover to the side.

"Molly?" Slater called out, looking down into the gaping hole in the ground.

The opening was definitely wide enough that a person could be shoved in there, but if Joelle's dad had had it capped up like this, it had to be deep. Probably deep enough to kill a person if they fell or were pushed in.

"Molly?" Slater shouted again.

No response. Not from the well, anyway. But Duncan heard something coming from the outbuilding. Not a voice but a barely audible thump. It was enough to get the three of them running toward it.

"Woodrow and Sonya, keep an eye on Joelle," Duncan told the deputies who had just come out of the barn. They'd obviously been searching it for more gunmen and Molly.

Slater reached the outbuilding first, and Ronnie and Duncan both readied their weapons while Slater threw open the door and then immediately darted to the side in case someone was about to fire at him.

But no shots came.

A sound did, though. Another of those thumps, and when Duncan looked inside, he saw Molly on the floor.

Alive.

Duncan couldn't add the "and well" part to that, though. Her eyes were wide. Her forehead, smeared with dirt and maybe even some blood. Her hair was a tangled halo around her face. But she was very much alive.

He quickly saw that Molly was gagged and tied up, and

she was bumping the side of her leg against the tire of an ATV, the only movement she could have managed, considering the way she was positioned in the shed. That bumping had likely caused the sounds they'd heard. They would have no doubt found her in the search, but that had allowed them to get to her even sooner.

Slater hurried to her, easing down her gag while Ronnie got to work on the ropes around her feet. Duncan called 911 for an ambulance. The moment the gag was off her mouth, Molly cried out in pain.

"Hospital," she managed to say. "I'm in labor."

Chapter Nine

The images came at Joelle hard and fast. The blood. So much blood. And it was on those photos she had seen in the yard at the ranch. The ones she'd been forced to walk through when the kidnapper had her.

Joelle groaned and tried to yank herself away from those images. She had to climb her way out of this nightmare because she couldn't be here. She couldn't—

"Joelle," someone said.

Duncan.

And she thought that was his hands on her arms. It was enough to yank her back, and her eyes flew open. Yes, Duncan. He was right there, hovering and looking very concerned.

"I'm okay," she managed to say. "It was just a nightmare."

A nightmare she'd lived when the kidnapper had her. Oh, this was going to stay with her for a while, and she didn't need any new horrific memories to blend with the others she already had.

"No, you're not okay," Duncan said, sitting beside her. "But you soon will be. Just level your breathing. In and out," he instructed.

She tried to do that. Tried, too, to push away the lingering bits of the dream. Then, she remembered the rest of what happened. Remembered where she was as well. She was in a hospital bed. Not because she'd been injured. No, both the baby and she were fine. The doctor had told her that during the exam he'd given her after they'd arrived at the hospital.

With Molly.

Molly wasn't okay. Joelle had seen the cuts and bruises on her face, and she remembered Molly had been in labor.

"Did Molly have the baby?" she asked. "Are they all right?"

"She's okay. She's still in labor so the baby hasn't come yet." He dragged in a weary breath, and there was plenty of worry on his face. Some of that worry was no doubt for her and their own child. "The doctors have assured me that six hours isn't that long when it comes to labor."

Six hours. That's how long it'd been, and Joelle realized she'd slept nearly a full hour of that. Well, slept and dreamed anyway.

"The last update I got was that Molly was about seven centimeters dilated," Duncan explained. "So, maybe it won't be long now." He paused a moment and eased a strand of hair off Joelle's cheek. "Molly's injuries aren't serious, thank God. And the baby seems to be perfectly fine."

Joelle felt the relief shove aside some of those remnants of the nightmare. "Good." And she repeated it several times.

"Obviously, we haven't been able to ask Molly about the kidnapping," Duncan went on. "There'll be time for that later after the baby's born."

She figured he was wishing he could question Molly since the woman might be able to tell them more than they already knew. And it occurred to her that Duncan might know a whole lot more than he had when she'd fallen asleep.

"Sonya is with Molly in labor and delivery," Duncan went on before she could ask him for an update on the investigation. "Sonya went to childbirth classes with her and is Molly's coach. It's possible Sonya and Molly have been talking in between contractions." He eased off the bed and lifted a white bag. "The hospital food didn't look that good so I had this delivered from the diner. A grilled chicken sandwich, a fruit cup and milk. You should eat."

Joelle's stomach growled at the mention of food, and she realized that despite everything that'd gone on, she was in fact hungry. Duncan took out the items he'd mentioned, laying them out on the rolling table that he pulled over.

Apparently, she wasn't the only one hungry because he took out another sandwich, a bag of chips and a bottle of water for himself. He hadn't gotten his usual can of Pepsi, though, and she suspected that was because he knew it was her favorite as well but that she'd given up soda for the duration of the pregnancy.

"You've been here the whole time I've been sleeping," she commented, already knowing the answer. Duncan wouldn't risk leaving her, not when there were those two gunmen still at large. "Did you get any rest?"

He tipped his head to the chair in the corner. "Some."

Which meant maybe a catnap at most. Since there was also a laptop on the chair, it likely meant he'd spent the bulk of those six hours working. Joelle felt a little guilty about that, but then she reminded herself that her resting had been necessary. Doctor's orders. Yes, she and the baby were all right, but the doctor had said some sleep would remedy the effects of stress caused by the attack.

They ate in silence for a few moments, but she didn't miss the glances he kept giving her. Often, she could pinpoint what was on Duncan's mind just by looking at him, but there had to be plenty on his mind right now. Joelle plucked out one of the possibilities.

"Have you managed to ID the man who tried to kill me?" she asked.

"Not yet."

She hadn't thought it possible, but just admitting that tightened his jaw even more. Of course, everything about this bothered him because the attacks were aimed at her which meant they were also aimed at the baby.

"And we had to let Hamlin go," Duncan added a moment later. "I can't prove he didn't send that fake text to himself. Hell, I can't prove anything that'll land him in jail."

Yes, definitely plenty of frustration mixed with the worry and exhaustion. Not a good mix.

"Did you see the photos of my father in the yard?" she added.

Of course, she knew that he had. He wouldn't have missed something that big at a crime scene, and even though he'd left with her to follow Molly in the ambulance, Duncan had likely gotten a glimpse of them. He'd probably had more than a glimpse by now since one of the other deputies would have bagged them for processing and sent him pictures of them.

He nodded and continued to study her. "The man we have in custody won't talk about them, but I'm guessing he's the one who put them there. Is that what caused you to drive the cruiser to that part of the yard?"

It was Joelle's turn to nod. And to wince and shake her head. "It was a trap, and I fell for it. He was right there, hiding, waiting for me."

"If you hadn't driven over to them, he likely would have just come after you where you were parked," Duncan was quick to point out. "It was a risky plan, what with cops and ranch hands all over the place."

Yes, it had been risky. And it'd nearly worked.

"The man was wearing Kevlar beneath his shirt," Duncan went on, "but he could have been shot elsewhere if someone had spotted him charging at you."

That was also true. "Does that make him an idiot, cocky or desperate?" she wanted to know.

"Maybe all three." He took a bite of his sandwich, motioned for her to do the same, and she did. "His name is Willie Jay Prescott," he added after he'd washed the bite down with some of his water. "At least we think that's his name. The lab got a match on the blood found at Molly's, and it belongs to this Willie Jay. Since the guy who tried to take you had a cut on his arm, we're guessing Molly wounded him and he left some blood behind."

That made sense. Well, maybe it did. "There were at least three gunmen involved in the combined attack on me and in Molly's kidnapping," Joelle reminded him.

He made a quick sound of agreement. "When I'm able to talk to Molly, I'll show her Willie Jay's picture and ask if he was the one with her the whole time. It's possible he wore a mask around her, but she might be able to ID him."

Since Molly was a former cop, Joelle was betting the woman would be able to do it, too. Even though Molly would have been terrified during her captivity, she would have no doubt paid attention to the man holding her.

"My father's killer or his accomplice is probably the one who took those photos," she said. Again, this wouldn't be a surprise to Duncan. "That means Willie Jay could have been the one who murdered him?"

"Possibly." Duncan added a heavy sigh to that response. "But it could have been someone else. I'll try to come up with a way to get Willie Jay to open up about that. Hell, to open up about anything because right now, he's refusing to say a word."

"Has he lawyered up?" she asked.

"Not so far, but he also won't confirm he even understands his rights. That means a psych eval. I've already scheduled one to give the official determination that he's competent enough to be charged with kidnapping, forced imprisonment, attempted kidnapping of another police officer and any other charge I can tack onto that."

The attempted kidnapping charges would definitely stick since there were plenty of witnesses. A crime like that would send him to jail for a long time. But it'd be a heck of a lot longer if they could prove he'd been the one to take and hold Molly.

And if he'd killed her father.

She doubted Willie Jay was just going to confess to that.

"We could maybe build a circumstantial case for murder if we can connect Willie Jay to those photos," she said, thinking out loud. "Because only the killer or someone who had knowledge of the killer would have those."

Even if Willie Jay was only an accomplice in that particular crime, it would carry the same penalty as the murder itself. Which would put Willie Jay on death row. Joelle wanted that. She wanted her father's killer to pay.

But she also wanted answers.

Why had her father been gunned down? And had Willie Jay orchestrated that, or was he merely a hired gun? Added to that, why had he wanted her? As she'd told Duncan earlier, he could have killed her, and he hadn't. He had intended to kidnap her. It was possible that was so he could get the baby, but there had to be an easier way to get his hands on a pregnant woman.

And that circled her back to the pictures.

Then, back to their suspects.

"If Brad, Kate or Hamlin are connected to Willie Jay," Joelle said, hoping this idea made sense when she spelled it out, "then, maybe you can use that as a trigger to get Willie Jay to talk. Maybe let Willie Jay believe you'll let one of them get access to him. *Bad access*," she emphasized. "As in the kind of access to have him murdered because he can link one of them to the attacks, Molly's kidnapping and my father's murder."

Of course, there was no way Duncan would actually allow a prisoner to be hurt or killed like that, but it might work if Willie Jay thought Duncan would do something that drastic. Judging from the sound Duncan made, he agreed.

"Willie Jay might tell us something that'll pinpoint who's responsible for what happened. Including your father's murder," he added. "Because I think it's highly likely that someone hired Willie Jay. There's nothing in his background to lead me to believe he's capable of putting together something like this. I could be wrong, but I don't think so."

Since Joelle hadn't had a chance to pour through what they'd learned about Willie Jay, Duncan's assessment was enough for her to believe the man was a lackey. It was his boss they wanted.

"What about Brad?" she asked as they continued to eat. "Is he still at the sheriff's office?"

Duncan shook his head. "His lawyer showed up and insisted Brad had to leave to make funeral arrangements for Shanda. Brad apparently broke down, and Carmen thought he might need to be sedated."

Joelle raised an eyebrow, and Duncan must have picked up on the question she was about to ask.

"I have no idea if Brad's grief is real," he said, "or if he's the one who killed Shanda, but since we had so much going on, I had Carmen reschedule the rest of the interview for tomorrow. Ruston arranged for some SAPD cops to tail Brad to make sure he doesn't try to flee. By the way, Ruston's on his way here to check on you."

She didn't groan, though Joelle hated that her brother was taking the time to do that. Especially since there were so many other things that needed to be done. But she also knew that talking Ruston out of a visit would be impossible. He was her big brother, and he no doubt felt an obligation to make sure she was all right.

"Kate is clamoring to get out of the hospital and go home," Duncan said a moment later, continuing the update of all three of their suspects. "She claims she's in danger." He lifted his shoulder. "She might be if Brad or Hamlin want her dead, and that's one of the reasons I'm keeping a deputy on her door."

Yes, and the other reason was to make sure Kate didn't leave before they had a chance to find out if she was the mastermind behind what was going on.

The silence came again. So did some memories. Recent ones. Or rather a recent *one*. And Joelle knew they needed to talk about it.

"I should apologize for kissing you," she said.

Duncan laughed. "Joelle, you never need to apologize for that. But I know where this is leading," he was quick to add. "Kissing me brings back a lot of bad stuff for you."

It did. But it brought back good stuff, too. Specifically, the heat. "It's a distraction neither of us need right now," she pointed out.

No way could Duncan disagree with that, but he certainly didn't jump to say she was right. "There are a lot of different distractions," he said, his gaze sliding to her stomach. "The baby's the top priority."

Joelle was thankful he'd spelled that out. Despite the bitter feelings between Duncan and her over her father's murder, she knew he was committed to this baby. That he loved her. And right now, Joelle very much needed that.

"I always figured when I had a baby, that my parents would be around to share the experience," she said. Of course, that brought on a wave of bitter memories. "They very much wanted to be grandparents."

"They did," Duncan muttered.

She heard something in his voice, some of his own bitter memories, and she thought this went beyond what'd happened in the past five months. Duncan hadn't had the loving childhood she had. Just the opposite. From the bits and pieces he'd told her, his bio-dad had never been in the picture, and when he'd been six, his junkie mother's boyfriend had killed her in a domestic dispute. Duncan ended up in foster care and bounced around from place to place until he landed with an elderly aunt who lived in Saddle Ridge. The aunt had died when Duncan was a senior in high school so he had no family to speak of.

Well, no family except this baby she was carrying.

"You'll be a good dad," she muttered.

It was the truth, but part of her wished she hadn't spelled it out like that. It broke down yet even more of the barriers between them. So did the look he gave her.

A long lingering look that started at her eyes and landed on her mouth.

Thankfully, they didn't have time to make the mistake of another kiss because there was a tap on the door, and Duncan practically came to attention. He moved away from the food, positioning himself between her and whoever opened the door a moment later. Duncan slid his hand over his gun. But it wasn't a threat.

Ruston stuck his head inside.

"Good," her brother said. "You're awake." Ruston glanced

at Duncan's stance and nodded his approval. "Glad you're here and taking precautions."

They had a suspect just up the hall and a possible missing gunman. Joelle figured there'd be a lot of precautions until they made some arrests.

Ruston went to her, helped himself to one of the grapes from her fruit cup, and then leaned down to kiss her cheek. He took hold of her chin, turning her face while he examined her. He frowned when his attention landed on the bruises on her neck and temple. The ones on the neck had happened when Willie Jay had put her in a choke hold. The other was from the barrel of his gun.

"The SOB will pay for that," Ruston snarled.

Joelle didn't huff or remind her brother that she was a cop and such things happened to those in law enforcement. Yes, she was a cop all right, but she would always be his little sister. So would Bree, even though there wasn't a wide age gap between any of them. Each of the McCullough offspring had been born two years apart with Ruston the oldest at thirty-seven. Slater, thirty-five. She was thirty-three, and Bree, the baby of the family, was thirty-one.

"I can give you something that I think will help you make the SOB pay," Ruston added to Duncan, and he took out his phone. "On the drive over here, one of the techs called me. Shanda didn't have security cameras, but there was one on the street."

Ruston pulled up something on his phone and held it out for them to see. It was the grainy image of a nondescript dark-colored car, but the graininess didn't extend to the part of the photo of the driver.

"Willie Jay," Duncan and she said in unison.

"Yep," Ruston verified. "This was taken just up the block from Shanda's house, and if you look at the time stamp, it means he was there right around the time Shanda was being murdered."

Joelle felt a welcome wave of relief. Willie Jay would end up in jail for a long time, maybe even on death row. But that wouldn't convict him of her father's murder. Not unless they found a connection.

"We have Willie Jay's gun," Duncan explained. "The lab can see if it's a match to the one used to kill Shanda."

"Good," Ruston muttered. "Since Shanda was murdered in San Antonio, SAPD will be charging Willie Jay with that, but I don't want him to go unpunished for what he did to Molly and Joelle. I'd like to see him convicted on all charges with the sentences running consecutively. That way, even if he doesn't get the death penalty, there'd be no chance that he'll ever see the outside of a jail cell."

Joelle got another wave of relief, but there was still that nagging thought running through her head. "I want to find a connection between Willie Jay and Dad's murder. He might have been the one to pull the trigger."

Since there was absolutely no surprise on Ruston's face, Joelle knew that had already occurred to him. Of course, it had. Ruston had probably read every report connected to what had happened.

"I'm working on it," Ruston assured her just as there was another knock at the door.

Like earlier, Duncan braced. So did Ruston. But it was Sonya who peered in, and the deputy was smiling.

"Molly had the baby," Sonya announced. "A perfectly healthy girl. Seven pounds, three ounces, and I can attest to the quality of her lungs because she yelled plenty when she finally came out."

Tears watered Joelle's eyes, but these were definitely of the happy variety. "How's Molly?"

"She's great." Sonya didn't seem to be lying about that, either. "She's totally in love already with her baby girl." Now she paused. "I think that'll help her get over the trauma of what happened."

"Did Molly talk about the kidnapping?" Duncan was quick to ask, but the question had also been on the tip of Joelle's tongue.

"Not much. And I didn't press her on it," Sonya admitted. "Molly mainly just wanted assurance that her kidnapper was behind bars. He still is, right?"

"He is," Duncan verified.

"Good. Because I'm sure Molly will ask when she sees you. You can see her now," Sonya added. "A really short visit, though, after the pediatrician is finished examining Annika. That's what Molly's naming her."

Joelle got up out of the bed, intending to head to see Molly right away, but Duncan's phone rang.

"It's Luca," Duncan relayed. "You're on speaker," he added to Luca when he answered. "Give me some good news."

"I might be able to do just that," Luca replied. "I've been digging into Willie Jay's background, and I found out something very interesting. Willie Jay used to work for one of our suspects."

Chapter Ten

Hamlin.

Duncan wouldn't have been surprised no matter which of their suspects Luca had named. Kate, Brad or Hamlin. At this point, Duncan considered the three to all be sharing that top spot for their number one suspect.

Too bad he couldn't eliminate two of them, and then he'd know which one of them was responsible. Well, maybe. The gut-twisting possibility was that the culprit hadn't even surfaced, that Willie Jay's boss was someone other than Hamlin.

Still, Willie Jay had worked for Hamlin so that was a start.

"Arrange to have Hamlin brought in right away," Duncan told Luca, and Luca assured him he'd do just that.

Duncan ended the call and slipped his phone back in his pocket. "Sonya, I figure you didn't get much rest, what with being called in early and Molly's birth coach, but do you have the bandwidth to stay here with the baby and her until I can get someone else to guard them?"

"I can stay as long as needed," Sonya quickly assured him. "In fact, I'd like to stay the night. Molly and I are friends, and I think she'd be more comfortable with me than with someone else."

"I agree," Duncan told her, "but if you feel yourself start to fade, then let me know."

Duncan checked the time. The hours were just racing by, and they had so much to do. But it was a priority now to see Molly. Not just because she might be able to give them answers but also because she was part of their Saddle Ridge Sheriff's Office family, and she'd been through a hellish ordeal. Then, Joelle and he could go back to the sheriff's office and wait for Hamlin. Duncan had no doubts that Luca would be able to locate the PI and get him in there fast.

"I take it you're up to this visit with Molly and the baby?" Duncan asked Joelle.

"Absolutely." Her answer was quick and resolute.

Ruston checked his watch as well, and he leaned over and brushed another kiss on Joelle's cheek. "I'll head back to San Antonio and work the arrest warrant there. I just wanted to see for myself that you were all right. Are you going to Slater's tonight or will you stay with Duncan?"

Obviously, the question threw her because she gave him a blank stare for a couple of seconds. "To be determined," she said at the same moment Duncan said, "I'll take her to my place."

"Good," Ruston concluded, but he didn't spell out why he felt that way.

"Good," Joelle murmured, not sounding nearly as pleased about staying with him as Ruston had been.

They went into the hall with Ruston heading for the exit, and Sonya, Duncan and her going in the direction of labor and delivery. Sonya must have sensed Duncan needed to have a word with Joelle about the sleeping arrangements because she walked ahead of them, giving them some privacy.

Duncan waited for Joelle to spell out that it was risky

for them to be under the same roof. Especially after the kiss and the steamy looks they'd been giving each other.

"My resistance for you is really low right now," she whispered. "You saved my life, and you're the father of a baby we both love and want to protect."

That was it. No extra line to clarify where that low resistance would lead them. Duncan's guess was to bed since he didn't have a whole lot of resistance when it came to her, either.

And that caused him to curse.

Because she'd just confessed she was vulnerable. Of course, she was. She'd nearly been kidnapped and could have been killed. So, landing in bed was totally out since it'd be taking advantage of her.

"Yes," she murmured when he cursed again, and the response confirmed she was well aware of his thought process.

His body didn't want to give up on the "landing in bed" part, but Duncan had to shove all thoughts of that aside as Sonya opened one of the hospital room doors. When Duncan looked in, he immediately saw Molly on the bed. She was smiling and cooing down at the baby she was holding.

"Isn't she beautiful?" Molly asked, her smile widening when she looked up at them.

Duncan took one of the paper surgical masks from a wall holder, put it on and went closer. "Yep, she's beautiful all right."

And she was. A perfect little face with fingers so tiny that Duncan hoped Molly didn't insist he hold her. She seemed way too fragile for that, but he got a reminder that soon, in four months or so, he'd have to get past that fear since he'd be holding his own child.

Joelle put on a mask and walked closer, peering down

at the baby. Even though Duncan couldn't see her expression, he knew she was smiling. "Molly, she's adorable." Joelle gave Molly's arm a gentle squeeze. "Congratulations, Mom."

"It's all a little daunting," Molly admitted, "and a whole lot amazing." She seemed ready to go on about the joys of motherhood. She didn't, though. She looked at Duncan. "You want to ask me questions about the kidnapping."

"Are you up to that?" he offered. "Because it can wait—"

"I can tell you what happened," Molly interrupted, "and then maybe we can do a more formal statement after I've gotten some sleep."

Duncan nodded and decided to let Molly say whatever it was she clearly wanted to say. If he saw her energy levels draining, then he would put a stop to this and come back.

Molly dragged in a long breath. "I was asleep when I heard my security system go off. I picked up my phone, thinking that maybe it was some kind of malfunction, but it wasn't. I heard someone moving around in my living room so I hit the last number I'd called. Joelle's. Then, I saw two men coming into my bedroom."

"Two?" Joelle asked.

Molly nodded. "They were both wearing ski masks, dark clothes. Both were about six feet and with somewhat muscular builds."

That described Willie Jay. Hell, it described a lot of men, and while Duncan was certain they had one of the kidnappers in custody—Willie Jay—they obviously needed to look for his partner. And Joelle's attacker. Of course, it was possible the second kidnapper was also the one who'd fired those shots into the cruiser at Joelle.

"I tried to get to my gun that I keep in the drawer next to the bed, but they grabbed me before I could do that,"

Molly went on. "I hit one of them with my phone and then dug my nails into his arm. I guess I cut him deep enough for him to leave blood at my house."

"We've identified that blood," Duncan told her. "Willie Jay Prescott. We have him in custody."

Molly's breath hitched, maybe from relief. "And the other?"

"We'll find him," he assured her, and Duncan hoped that was the truth. They needed to find the remaining person or persons responsible for this.

Molly paused a moment, kissed her daughter's cheek and then started again. "They put a hood over my head, tied up my hands and feet, and got me into a vehicle. A truck, I think, because of the way they had to lift me to put me in it. And they drove away."

It was hell for Duncan to hear all of this. To know the terror that had to have been going through Molly's mind. She'd probably thought she would lose her precious baby as well as her own life.

"The men didn't talk when we were driving," she went on. "But we weren't in the vehicle long. Maybe ten minutes or less."

Duncan calculated that was about the time it would have taken the kidnappers to get from Molly's house to the Mc-Cullough ranch. "Did they take you to the location where we found you, or did you go somewhere else first?"

"Just that one location. Your dad's ranch," Molly muttered, looking at Joelle. "I didn't know that's where I was until the EMTs were taking me to the ambulance."

That made Duncan do more mental cursing. All those hours, Molly had been so close. But they'd had so many places to search, and Molly hadn't had any connection to the McCullough ranch. She had been taken there because the kidnappers no doubt knew it was empty.

Molly cleared her throat before she continued, "After I was in the shed, I'm sure one of them left. The one who smelled like cinnamon stayed, and the other left."

"Cinnamon?" Duncan pressed.

Molly nodded. "He was chewing some kind of gum or candy. He's the one who made the calls to Joelle." She paused. "And I honestly believed what he was saying, that he regretted kidnapping me."

Maybe he did. But obviously Willie Jay hadn't felt that.

"A couple of hours before you found me," Molly continued, "the second man came back, and they had a whispered conversation. The cinnamon guy was pleading with the other to let me go, but the second man said no. They went out of the shed, and they argued, but I couldn't make out what they were saying. Then, neither one came back in. I didn't hear anyone else until you and the deputies showed up."

Duncan could only speculate as to what'd happened. Maybe the "cinnamon guy" had stormed off. Or maybe Willie Jay had eliminated him. If so, the man's body hadn't been found on the ranch, and the CSIs and some of his deputies had been combing the place.

"If you get me a sample of Willie Jay's voice, I should be able to confirm he was one of the kidnappers," Molly offered.

"I'll do that," he said just as the baby let out a kitten-like cry. That was his cue to leave and let Molly have some time with her daughter.

Joelle gave Molly another gentle hug, ran her fingers over the baby's cheek and left with Duncan. He was about to call Slater or Luca to provide backup while they went to the sheriff's office, but Slater was already in the hall, waiting for them.

"Ruston told me about Hamlin's connection to Willie Jay," Slater explained as they headed for the exit. "He's on his way in for an interview, but he's not happy."

"Welcome to the club," Duncan muttered. But in Hamlin's case, not being happy was a good thing. Riled people often said more than they intended to.

As expected, Slater had the cruiser waiting for them right outside the ER doors, and the three of them hurried to get in. Duncan glanced at Joelle and saw that she was looking at the window next to her. And she was no doubt recalling that Willie Jay had shot through a similar window to get to her.

The bullet-resistant glass was better than nothing, but this had to be a reminder that they weren't safe, not even in the cruiser. Duncan could only hope they'd be making an arrest soon that would put an end to the danger.

Duncan kept watch as Slater drove, but he didn't see anyone he didn't recognize. If Joelle hadn't been with him and if they hadn't been in the middle of town, Duncan would have wanted to spot the missing attacker. Would have liked to have a showdown with him. But the thug apparently wasn't showing his face in broad daylight.

After Slater parked, they went into the sheriff's office. Which was nearly bare. Understandable, what with all the various components of the investigation going on and with some of the deputies needing rest after a hellishly long day. Woodrow was at his desk, working on his laptop, and Ronnie was at his. Not alone. There was a young brunette woman sitting next to him. Both Ronnie and the woman got to their feet, their attention turning to Duncan.

"This is Erica Corley," Ronnie said. "She just came in to talk to you."

The name was familiar, but Duncan thumbed through his memory to figure out if he recognized her. He didn't. And when Joelle and Slater shook their heads, he figured they didn't know her, either.

"I'm Sheriff Holder." Duncan went closer to Erica and hitched a thumb at Joelle and Slater when he introduced them.

The woman nodded, swallowed hard. "I'm Al Hamlin's ex-girlfriend. Al and I had a baby together when we were teenagers."

Duncan was certain he looked surprised because he was. Not about the baby part but that Erica would just show up like this. Then again, it was possible the PI they'd talked to had located her and sent her to them.

"I heard about the kidnapping and attacks on the news," Erica went on. "One of the reports mentioned Al, that he was on the scene when a man was taken into custody."

Duncan silently groaned. He didn't know how the media picked up on such details, but he had to admit a story like this would make good press.

"And I thought… Well, I wondered," Erica added a moment later, "if Al was involved in some way?"

Since that was exactly what Duncan wanted to know, he motioned for Erica to go into his office. Joelle came, too, but Slater muttered something about needing to check for updates, and he headed to his desk in the bullpen.

"Can I get you some coffee or water?" Duncan asked her.

Erica shook her head and took one of the seats next to Duncan's desk. Joelle took the other.

"Was Al involved in the kidnapping and attacks?" Erica pressed.

Considering that Willie Jay had worked for Hamlin, the answer was yes, but Duncan kept that to himself and went with a question of his own. "Do you believe your ex is capable of something like that?" He'd asked Brad's ex, Shanda, the same thing, and she'd more or less waffled on her response.

Erica didn't.

"I believe he's capable," she said after a heavy sigh. "I don't know why he'd do it, but…" She stopped. "It could be because of what happened with our baby. I suppose you know about that?"

"We do," Duncan verified.

Erica nodded. "I wanted to give the baby up for adoption, and Al wanted to, well, sell it."

There was some anger, maybe even shame, in those last few words, and Erica lowered her head, shook it.

"I was against it," Erica went on after several moments. "But Al kept pressing me. He said he'd gotten in touch with someone, and the person would pay us ten thousand dollars. I don't come from money, and that sounded like a fortune to me. So I went through with meeting with this person, even though I wasn't sure I could actually sell my child."

That meshed with what Duncan had read in the juvenile records that Slater had managed to get. The arresting officer had mentioned that Hamlin had been the one to orchestrate the sale and had also contacted the couple two more times to up the amount he wanted them to pay for the child. That's how the extortion had come into play.

The wannabe adoptive parents had been charged, too, since they had planned on paying for the baby, but no one involved in the case had pointed the finger at Erica as being the aggressor in the sale or the extortion. Still, she'd been convicted since she had gone along with meeting the couple.

"What happened at the meeting?" Joelle prompted when the woman fell silent.

Erica gave another of those long sighs. "The San Antonio cops found out what Al and I were doing because they showed up and arrested us." She shifted her attention to Joelle. "I think your late father was the one who told the cops."

Duncan didn't know who was more surprised by that, Joelle or him. "My father?" she questioned.

"I spoke to Sheriff Cliff McCullough shortly after I was arrested. He'd gotten a tip from a longtime confidential informant that a couple was trying to buy a baby, and he gave SAPD the couple's names, and that in turn put the cops on Al and me. We didn't even make it to the meeting with the couple because they in turn told the cops about us. We were convicted of attempted extortion and trying to sell the baby."

Joelle stayed quiet a moment. "Did Hamlin know about my father's involvement in this?"

"Sure," Erica was quick to say. "Your father spoke to both Al and me after the arrest. I'm not sure what he said to Al, but your dad was kind to me. He knew my folks had kicked me out, that I had no place to go and had been staying with friends just to have a roof over my head. He told me if I needed help with a legal adoption agency or if I decided to keep the baby, he could find me a place to go."

That part didn't surprise Duncan one bit. Sheriff McCullough had been a good man, and he would have done whatever possible to right a bad situation. If Erica was telling the truth, and Duncan believed she was, then her situation had definitely qualified as bad.

"I took the sheriff up on his offer," Erica explained. "I got out of juvie three months before Al did, and the sheriff helped me get into a home that had other girls like me.

I had the baby, legally put her up for adoption and then the sheriff arranged for me to get my GED and a job."

Joelle and Duncan exchanged glances, and he could practically see the wheels turning in her head. "How did Hamlin take that?"

"Not well." That answer was also quick. "He didn't find me until after I'd had the baby, and he was furious. Not because he wanted the child. But because he still thought I should have gotten some money for the baby. Money that I should have shared with him." Her bottom lip trembled a little. "I told Al to leave me alone or I'd ask Sheriff Mc-Cullough to help me file a restraining order against him."

Duncan figured Hamlin wasn't happy about that, either. In fact, it could have riled him to the core. Did it rile him enough, though, to carry on a vendetta to murder the sheriff and go after Joelle? Maybe. And maybe Molly played into the plan simply because she would soon give birth to a baby that Hamlin could sell.

Erica lifted her head and met Duncan's gaze. "I think Al might have pressured his sister to sell her child. That might be why Isla disappeared."

Duncan considered that for a moment and then tried to link that to what was happening now. If Hamlin had continued to dabble in selling babies, then it's possible Isla would have run from him.

"Did Al ever mention Kate Moreland?" Duncan asked.

Erica opened her mouth to answer, but the sound of a man's voice stopped her. Speaking of the devil, Hamlin came in, pushing his way past one of the deputies, and his attention must have landed on Erica.

"What the hell is she doing here?" Hamlin demanded.

Erica sprang to her feet, and Duncan thought the woman might cower in fear at the sight of her ex, but she turned and faced him head-on. "I came because I thought you might be involved in what happened to Deputy McCullough and the woman who was kidnapped."

Hamlin cursed, and he opened his mouth as if about to unleash some rage and profanity, but he quickly bit that off. He turned around, pacing a few steps, and when he turned back toward Erica, he scrubbed his hand over his face.

"Don't you see?" he asked her. "They'll use anything you've told them to try and pin these crimes on me. I'm just trying to find my sister and make the people who took her pay."

"I had to come," Erica fired back. There was no real anger in her voice, just that shamed reaction again. "I don't know for sure if you've had any part in what happened, but I wanted to tell the sheriff about our arrest. I didn't think it would come up in a normal search since we were underage."

"And it's irrelevant," Hamlin insisted. He snapped toward Duncan and repeated that. "Yes, I was convicted of doing something very stupid by trying to get money for our child. I was young and desperate, and I made a mistake. All of that has nothing to do with the attacks. I told you I was there on scene because I got a text from you. Or rather a text I thought was from you."

"It wasn't," Duncan verified. And that's why Duncan had had his phone records entered into the investigation log so it would be clear he hadn't been the one who'd messaged Hamlin telling him to go to the McCullough ranch. According to the techs, the message had come from a burner, which meant Hamlin could have sent it to himself.

That was a reminder of why Duncan had wanted Hamlin to be interviewed, but he wasn't sure if Erica had more to add to the investigation or not. "Thank you for coming in today," Duncan told the woman. "Deputy Slater Mc-

Cullough will take your statement because there are some things I have to ask Hamlin."

And Duncan didn't want to do that in front of Erica. He needed to keep this all by the book since he soon might be charging Hamlin with a boatload of felonies.

Duncan tipped his head to the interview room. "This way," he told Hamlin, and Joelle followed in step behind them. On the short walk, Duncan repeated the Miranda warning.

Hamlin muttered throughout the warning, and he was still muttering when they were in the room and seated. "Erica shouldn't have come and stirred up things like that," he snapped. "I had nothing to do with what happened to Deputy McCullough and the dispatcher."

"Nothing to do with Sheriff Cliff McCullough, either?" Duncan threw out there.

Hamlin flinched. Then, he huffed again. "Erica told you that the sheriff is the one who ratted us out. Yes, he did. He poked his nose into something that wasn't his business, but I'm going to repeat myself again. I had nothing to do with what's been going on."

Duncan just stared at the man, and after a few seconds had crawled by, he said, "Willie Jay Prescott." And he watched Hamlin's reaction.

Joelle was no doubt watching, too, which meant she saw the flicker of recognition in Hamlin's eyes. "Want to tell us about your relationship with Willie Jay?" she suggested, though it was more of an order.

Hamlin's mouth tightened, and he belted out some more profanity. "What about him?"

Duncan huffed. "Stop playing games with us. Willie Jay is in a jail cell right here in this building, and he's had plenty to say."

Of course, that last part was a lie. Willie Jay hadn't said a word, but it was obvious that the revelation of Willie Jay's arrest put some serious concern on Hamlin's face.

Hamlin stayed quiet a moment, his gaze flickering right and then left. "Mr. Prescott briefly worked for me when I first became a PI," he finally said. "I employed him to help me track down leads on my cases. The employment didn't last because Mr. Prescott turned out to be not very reliable at showing up for work or doing his assigned tasks. So, I fired him."

Duncan continued to fix his hard stare on the man. "When was this?"

Hamlin certainly wasn't quick to answer. "I officially fired him about two months ago, but he hasn't actually worked for me in nearly a year. I just quit giving him assignments." He paused a heartbeat, and some more anger flared through his eyes. "Mr. Prescott was *not* happy about me terminating his employment so I'm sure anything he told you is to get back at me for firing him."

Duncan made a sound to indicate he was giving that some thought and he shook his head. "He didn't mention anything about you firing him." And Duncan left it at that, letting Hamlin squirm.

He squirmed all right and did more cursing. "Look, I don't know what Willie Jay said about me, but I've done nothing illegal. Nothing illegal since that incident when I was a teenager," he amended when Duncan lifted an eyebrow. "The person you should be looking at is Kate Moreland. She's behind these attacks."

"So you've said," Duncan commented. "But I'm not seeing a whole lot of proof that she's guilty. You, on the other hand, have a strong connection to a hired thug, Willie Jay, who we caught red-handed. He's going down, and he's going down hard. It'll be interesting to see who he takes with him."

The anger came again, like a burst of red-hot heat, but it faded just as quickly. "The person he should be taking down with him is Kate because I didn't hire Willie Jay to go after Deputy McCullough or your dispatcher."

Joelle leaned in. "Why are you so sure it's Kate? There has to be more to this vendetta of yours—"

"She was the one who contacted me when I was seventeen and Erica was pregnant," Hamlin blurted. "I'd been asking around, and she got in touch with me. She called herself a middleman in the process. A *facilitator* was the word she used."

Interesting. Because Kate hadn't mentioned anything about that. Then again, this might all be Hamlin blowing smoke.

"Kate contacted you personally?" Duncan asked.

Hamlin nodded. "With a phone call. I'd left my number around in case anyone was interested. I spelled out that Erica and I wanted some money to cover the expenses of her pregnancy and the upcoming delivery."

Duncan raised his eyebrow again.

"All right." Hamlin huffed. "I wanted more than expenses covered. I wanted to be able to give Erica and me a fresh start. And she had already said she was giving up the baby. It wasn't as if I pressured her to do that."

Maybe. Duncan figured some pressure was involved once Hamlin realized he could get money for the baby. Still, Duncan didn't want to muddy this line of questioning.

"So, did you actually meet with Kate when you were trying to arrange for the sale of your child?" Duncan asked.

The wording clearly riled Hamlin, but Duncan wasn't planning on sugarcoating anything. "No," Hamlin snarled.

"Then you can't know for certain it was Kate More-land," Joelle was quick to point out. She obviously wasn't sugarcoating, either.

"It was her," Hamlin insisted, but then he paused and seemed to have a lightbulb over the head moment. "It was her voice. I've heard recordings of her speaking at various social events, and I'm positive it was Kate."

"Maybe," Duncan repeated.

"There's no maybe to it. It was Kate, and after that ini-tial call, I dealt with one of her employees."

That got Duncan's attention. "Who?"

"A man named Arlo Dennison," Hamlin said without hesitation. "I've researched him, and he used to manage one of her gyms. He doesn't any longer. In fact, he's not offi-cially on her payroll that I can find, but she's probably pay-ing him under the table for more black market baby deals."

"That's possible," Duncan admitted. "But other things fall into the area of possibilities, too. For instance, you're the one doing the baby-brokering deals, and you want to toss some bad light on Kate so she'll take the heat for some-thing you're doing."

Yeah, it was a hard push, but Duncan had wanted to see how Hamlin would react. And he saw all right. Ham-lin got to his feet.

"I'm going to terminate this interview right now and come back with a lawyer," Hamlin insisted. He glared at Duncan. "Unless you plan on arresting me simply because I once employed a man you now have in custody."

Duncan wished he could arrest Hamlin. It'd take one of their prime suspects off the street. But there was no way he could get an arrest warrant much less a conviction with what he had.

"Come back first thing in the morning with your lawyer," Duncan told Hamlin. "By first thing, I mean eight o'clock. Be here or I'll send someone to bring you in."

Of course, that riled Hamlin even more, and the man stormed out. Duncan immediately took out his phone to look up this Arlo Dennison, but Joelle had already done it.

"Arlo Dennison," she relayed, "is forty-two and did, indeed, manage one of Kate's gyms. He's got a sheet, an old one for assault and extortion. That was eleven years ago, so he either learned his lesson or he's gotten better at covering up his crimes. I'm texting you his number now," she added.

The moment Duncan's phone dinged with the text, he clicked on the number to call Arlo Dennison. There was a single ring before the call went to voice mail. The greeting was automated and simply told the caller to leave a message. Duncan didn't, though if Arlo checked his phone, he'd be able to figure out that the sheriff of Saddle Ridge was calling him.

"Arlo lives in San Antonio," Joelle added. "You want me to have Ruston send someone out to pick him up and bring him in for questioning?"

Duncan thought about it for a couple of seconds and nodded. "See if Ruston or another SAPD cop can do the interview."

That would save them from having to wait around for Arlo to come in. Duncan figured Joelle was spent for the day. He certainly was, and added to that, they would need to re-interview Kate and try to get Willie Jay to talk.

Joelle nodded and immediately called her brother. She'd barely had time to convey what they wanted when Duncan's own phone rang, and he saw Luca's name on the screen.

"We have a problem," Luca said the moment Duncan answered the call on speaker.

"What?" Duncan asked after he groaned.

"Woodrow found a truck on one of the ranch trails that's near the McCullough ranch. Inside it, there were two dead bodies."

Chapter Eleven

Two dead bodies.

Hearing Luca say that had given Joelle an initial hit of adrenaline. But that had been six hours ago. Now she was just wiped out and had to force herself to stay alert and focused as Duncan read the latest update he'd just gotten from Woodrow and the CSIs.

"Two males," Duncan said. He was standing behind his desk, reading from his laptop. "Both were identified through prints since they had criminal records. Darrin Finney, forty-two, from San Antonio, has a sheet for B&E, assault and drug possession. Troy Oakley, thirty-six, from Austin, has a nearly identical sheet, minus the drugs. The deaths were set up to look like a murder-suicide with Troy being the killer."

Joelle, who was seated in the chair, looked up at Duncan. "Set up?" she questioned.

Duncan nodded. "There was a note left at the scene, but the CSIs said the angles of the kill shots were wrong for it to have gone down that way."

He turned his laptop so she could read the note that had been photographed. The handwriting was basically a scrawl so it took her a moment to make out what it said. "Too many cops after us," she read aloud. "This is better than going to prison. We were wrong to go after that deputy and the other woman."

Even without the wrong angles of the kill shots, Joelle would have suspected the murder-suicide was a ruse. Sometimes, criminals did do things like this, but the truth was the cops weren't on the trails of these two. Their names hadn't even surfaced so far during the investigation.

"Both men had GSR on them," Duncan continued. "And Darrin Finney had some cinnamon gum in his pocket."

Continuing to fight the fatigue, Joelle considered that a moment. Molly had said one of her kidnappers chewed that particular flavor of gum so that probably meant these two were the ones who'd taken her.

"The truck they were in was reported stolen earlier today," Duncan added a moment later, "and there doesn't seem to be a connection between the owner of the vehicle and either of these two dead men."

Molly had also mentioned she believed they had transported her in a truck. So that matched as well.

"These two took Molly," Joelle summarized. "Maybe they did, anyway. Since Willie Jay ended up at the ranch with Molly, he could have been one of her initial kidnappers." She paused. "And that would mean the two worked together with someone else to cover both her kidnapping and the attack aimed at me. The *someone else* could be just one person. Or two."

"Probably two," Duncan said. "Because I don't believe they'd see going after a cop as a one man job. So, with two dead and one in custody, there's almost certainly someone else out there we need to find."

"You're thinking the fourth man might be this Arlo Dennison Hamlin told us about?" she asked.

Duncan shrugged and then sighed. She wasn't exactly

sure the reason for the sigh until he closed his laptop and walked around the desk to take her by the arm.

"I'm taking you to my place," he said, lifting her from the chair.

Part of her wanted to argue, to try to continue to push through the avalanche of information they'd gotten on this investigation. But the baby moved just as she opened her mouth to insist she had another couple of hours in her. She didn't. And the baby was a reminder that she had already had too much stress on her body today and she needed rest.

Duncan let go of her arm once they got moving out of his office and into the bullpen. Slater, Woodrow and Luca were all there. All still working. And that gave Joelle some fresh guilt over leaving when they hadn't. Still, the exhaustion wasn't giving her much of a choice about this.

Slater and Woodrow were both on the phone so Duncan turned to Luca. "Could you follow Joelle and me to my place?"

Luca's nod was quick. "You want me to stay there with you tonight?"

Duncan considered that for a moment and nodded. "Three of the attackers are out of commission, but I believe there's a fourth one and their boss are still out there. Let's go in one cruiser."

Luca nodded as well, and after mouthing the plan to Slater, he grabbed his laptop and went out the door first with Joelle and Duncan right behind them. Following their recent travel patterns, Duncan rode shotgun and Joelle took the back seat.

It wasn't far to Duncan's house, only about two miles, but travel anywhere wasn't exactly a breeze because of the attacks. All three of them knew any time out in the open could lead to another one. Added to that, it was dark now so someone could be lying in wait.

While Luca drove and they kept watch, Joelle tried to recall if Duncan had more than one guest room. Even though Duncan had owned the small ranch for five years now, she hadn't been to his place that often. Mainly because they'd spent a good chunk of those five years keeping their distance from each other.

Clearly, they'd ultimately failed since she was carrying his baby.

From the handful of visits she had made to his ranch, she recalled the house being fairly large, but even without guest rooms, she figured they'd all end up getting some sleep somewhere in the house since they had all been going at this for way too many hours.

Duncan's phone dinged with a text. A sound that instantly put Joelle on alert in case it was a message about an attack being imminent. She tried to hold onto the hope, though, that it was good news.

"It's from Slater," Duncan relayed to them. "SAPD uncovered something interesting on Kate. About three months ago, she accused Brad and Shanda of drugging her. She talked to a detective about it, and he investigated, but nothing came of it since there were no drugs in her system when Kate came in to report it."

Joelle worked that through in her mind. "I can see this playing out two ways. Either Brad and/or Shanda did, indeed, drug the woman. Or else Kate was laying the groundwork to set them up for the attacks she was planning on Molly and me."

Duncan made a sound of agreement. "And that takes us back to Kate's motive. If the attacks are to set someone up, why not do that to Hamlin? That would get him off her back."

"True," Joelle admitted. "But maybe her motive is about getting revenge for what happened to Shanda. I know she hated Shanda," she quickly added, "but the arrest and miscarriage ultimately caused a rift between Kate and her son. Kate would want to get back at Molly and me for that, and in the process she could end up with two babies to sell."

The thought of that sickened Joelle. Kate could possibly want to use her baby and Molly's to settle an old score.

It didn't take long, less than five minutes, before Luca took the turn into Duncan's driveway, and Duncan used his phone to open his garage door. He also turned on some security lights. Lots of them at both the front and sides of the house.

Unlike her place, Duncan had neighbors—a small-time rancher directly across the road from him and another about two hundred yards to his right. Not exactly right next door but close enough that the lights from those two places also provided some illumination as well.

Luca pulled into the garage, and they all stayed inside the cruiser until Duncan had shut the garage door behind them. "I have a security system," he said, checking his phone. "And I would have gotten an alert had someone gone into the house. Still, I want to do a sweep of the place just in case someone hacked into the system."

That wasn't exactly a comforting thought, but Joelle was glad Duncan had even considered it. The problem with being so tired was that it could cause a loss of focus on something critical like this.

Duncan got out, and he searched the garage first before he went into the house. Luca and she sat in the cruiser, waiting and hoping that all was well. They'd already been through way too much. Ditto for Molly, but Joelle had talked to the woman about an hour ago, and the baby and the new mother seemed to be doing well.

"Have you heard from Bree?" Luca asked, drawing Joelle's attention back to him.

"Yes. She's planning on coming home soon." Though now that she'd given that some thought, Joelle would try to talk her sister out of it. Saddle Ridge just wasn't a safe place to be right now.

Luca made a sound that could have meant anything, but Joelle thought she detected some kind of undercurrent. And she knew why. At best, Bree usually managed to come home three or four times a year and then for only a week or two.

The exception to that "coming home" pattern had been five months ago when their father had been murdered and their mother had disappeared. Bree had then stayed in Saddle Ridge for just over five weeks. Joelle knew that Bree and Luca had seen each other then, but there seemed to be some kind of rift between them and then Bree left. Luca might be wondering if he could fix that rift and go back to the way things had been.

That was a reminder for Joelle that she needed to have a conversation with Bree. Maybe soon if the fourth gunman wasn't caught and his boss arrested. Willie Jay could speed up the possibility of that if he'd just start talking. Arlo Dennison might be able to do that as well if the cops managed to find him. So far, that hadn't happened, which led Joelle to believe that he, too, might be dead.

Duncan finally appeared in the doorway that led into the house and motioned for them to come in. That helped ease some of the tension in Joelle's body. So did Duncan rearming the security system the moment they were inside.

"All the doors and windows have sensors," Duncan explained. "Normally, I keep the alarms at a soft beep since I'm a light sleeper, but I'll change that to a full sound. If someone tries to get in, we'll hear it."

Good. That was one less thing to worry about, especially since Molly's kidnappers had broken into her place despite her having a security system.

"This way," Duncan instructed. He led them through a kitchen with stainless appliances and white stone countertops. "Help yourself to anything in the fridge. Sorry that it isn't better stocked, but I hadn't counted on... Well, I hadn't counted on this."

Since Duncan had been steadily feeding her throughout the day, Joelle wasn't hungry, but she figured she would be by morning.

Duncan continued to lead them through the living and dining rooms and toward the hall. He stopped outside the first door. "It's my office, but there's a sofa sleeper," he said to Luca. "Bathroom is there." He tipped his head to the room directly across from the office.

Luca muttered a thanks, one weary with fatigue, and went in while Duncan continued with her to the next room. "Guest room," he explained, walking in with her. The walls and the comforter on the queen-size bed were both pale blue. "I'll be right next door. The walls are thin enough that I'll hear you if you call out."

Joelle sighed, hoping there'd be no need for her to call out, that nothing else would go wrong tonight.

Duncan stayed put, studying her for several moments. "This is probably going to sound wrong, but we can sleep together if that'll help with the tension that I can practically see coming off you in waves. *Sleep*," he emphasized.

Even though it was the worst reaction, Joelle smiled.

She should have instead given him a firm look to let him know she'd be fine in here alone. But she was out of firm looks for the night. She sighed again, then shook her head.

"Tempting, but I'll be okay," she muttered. She hoped. It was possible she was too tired and had too much firing through her head to actually sleep.

The corner of Duncan's mouth lifted. Apparently, he was going for his own *worst reaction*. He compounded that by pulling her into his arms.

Her body landed against his. Familiar territory for both of them. Bad territory, too, because it instantly spurred some memories that shouldn't be spurred right now. Their defenses were down. They were both vulnerable. Yet, neither one of them pulled away from each other.

Joelle actually moved in closer, sliding her arms around his waist and dropping her head onto his shoulder. Mercy, it felt good. Not just because of the heat but because of the comfort this gave her. She wasn't a weak woman. Definitely wasn't a coward. But it felt good to be this close to someone who had her back.

She felt Duncan brush a kiss on the top of her head. Not really any kind of foreplay per se, but anything they did at this point would qualify as foreplay. Again, that was a good reason for her to move away from him,

But she didn't.

Joelle lifted her head, came up on her tiptoes and kissed him. It wasn't an especially heated kiss, but it shouldn't have happened at all. Nothing about this could stay at the comforting level. It never would between Duncan and her. The heat that stirred between them would never allow a comfort level. It would only demand to be sated.

That didn't stop her from fully kissing him. Nor did it stop him from returning the kiss and tightening his arms around her, pulling her even closer to him. Until they were touching in all the wrong places.

Duncan used his foot to shut the bedroom door, and he was the one who deepened the kiss. Joelle didn't do anything to stop that, either. In fact, she welcomed it. Needed it. She needed him, and that made the situation even more dangerous. This kind of need wouldn't just rip down barriers, it would put a permanent end to them.

That still didn't stop her.

She slid her hand around his neck, pulling his mouth down to hers so she could deepen the kiss as well. So she could take. And burn. Oh, yes. She was burning all right, and the heat continued to skyrocket when he dropped his grip to her bottom and aligned them in just the right way.

Of course, the baby bump didn't allow for the usual direct body to body contact in their midsections, but it was plenty enough for Joelle to recall in perfect detail just how good this could be between Duncan and her. Good but with serious consequences. Remembering those consequences gave her just enough steel to ease her mouth from his.

Duncan stared down at her and blinked as if trying to clear his head, and then he muttered some profanity. "I didn't think," he said. "I didn't think of the baby."

He had created a wonderful steamy heat inside her head so it took a moment to cut through that and realize what he meant. She had to smile again.

"Pregnant women are allowed to kiss," she pointed out. "And have sex."

That last part flew right out of her mouth before she even knew she was going to say it. *Stupid, stupid, stupid.* Of course, it made Duncan smile again, and Joelle gave up and smiled right along with him.

The moment seemed to freeze. Their gazes certainly

did while they were locked with each other. And the heat came at them like an out-of-control train. Cutting through what was left of any common sense.

There was a ringing sound that cut through as well, and it had Duncan and her flying apart. For one horrifying moment, Joelle thought it was the security system alerting them that someone had broken in. But it was Duncan's phone.

"It's Slater," he said when he looked at the screen and put the call on speaker. She started to move away from him, but Duncan kept his arm around her waist.

"Hope I caught you before you crashed for the night," Slater greeted.

"You did," Duncan said. "Did you get something?"

"Yes." Slater stopped, cursed. "Shortly after you left, Willie Jay got a phone call. From Kate Moreland."

"Kate?" Duncan questioned. "What did she want?"

"She wouldn't say, but I told Willie Jay she'd called and tried to get him to tell me why she wanted to talk to him. He stayed clammed up. So, I went back to my desk to see if I could get the answer from Kate. She clammed up as well and said she had to go, that the doctor ordered her to rest."

Clearly, Duncan and she would be having a chat with Kate first thing in the morning.

"I dug deeper, looking for a connection between Willie Jay and Kate," Slater went on. Joelle could hear some chatter in the background at the sheriff's office. "When I got nothing, I went to check on Willie Jay, to see if he'd changed his mind about talking to us. He was unconscious when I found him." Her brother cursed again. "Duncan, Willie Jay's dead."

Chapter Twelve

Duncan poured himself another cup of coffee—his third of the morning—in the hope that it would help get rid of the headache that was throbbing at his temples and behind his eyes. That was a lot to ask of mere caffeine, but he needed a much clearer head than he had right now.

He heard the shower going in the guest room and figured Joelle would be out soon to join him in the kitchen. Maybe she'd gotten some sleep after he'd left her in the guest room an hour or so after Slater had called with the news about Willie Jay. Maybe. But like him, she'd obviously had to try to get that sleep while processing what the hell had happened.

Duncan was still processing that.

Luca no doubt was, too, because he had downed multiple cups of coffee since getting up and was now at the other end of the kitchen table while he worked on his laptop.

Like Duncan, the deputy was digging for anything and everything that would help them make sense of this. Joelle had almost certainly done the same. She just hadn't surfaced for coffee yet, probably because she could no longer have a morning jolt of caffeine. The pregnancy had apparently put a temporary halt to that.

"The tox report came in," Luca announced just as Duncan

saw it pop into his inbox. As promised, Slater had pressed the lab hard to get those results ASAP. No easy feat since it had taken the ME nearly two hours to arrange for the body to be removed from the jail and transported to the county morgue.

Duncan was scanning through those results when Joelle came hurrying into the kitchen. Her focus was on her phone screen, and her hair was damp, but she was dressed. She was wearing the clothes she'd washed and dried the night before after she'd borrowed one of his shirts and a pair of boxers to sleep in. Once they'd gotten the news about Willie Jay, Joelle had known she wouldn't want to be scrounging up some loaner clothes today, that she'd want to focus on the investigation.

"You saw the tox report," she said after glancing at them.

Duncan made a sound of agreement. "Cyanide in the form of a capsule." Part of the capsule had still been in his mouth. "Since Willie Jay was searched before he was locked up, that means he must have had the pill concealed somewhere on him. And that he must have intended to end his life rather than spend time in jail."

That, in turn, added slightly more credence to the murder-suicide of the other two gunmen. The angles of the shots were still off, but now Duncan had to consider that the men had been willing participants in their deaths.

Why?

That's what both Luca and he were digging to find out. Joelle likely would be doing that, too.

"We start with Kate. I want to find out why she called Willie Jay last night," Duncan said, checking the time. It was nearly eight o'clock. "I've already called Dr. Benton, and he said Kate had a rough night and requested sedation. But we'll be talking to her this morning."

That seemed to be Joelle's cue to get moving to the fridge, and she grabbed an apple, and after checking to see there was no milk or yogurt, she went with some cheese. "Did Dr. Benton say anything about what had caused Kate's rough night?"

"More or less. He told Kate that she'd be going home today. She asked if the deputy guarding her would be going with her, and the doctor said he didn't think so, but he didn't know for sure. He said she became agitated after hearing that and insisted she'd be in danger if she left the hospital. He left her for a while because he had to see another patient, and when he came back, she asked for the sedative."

"Does the timing work for when Kate would have tried to call Willie Jay?" Joelle asked.

"According to Benton, it does, and he said she was holding her phone when he came back in the room." Duncan paused. "And speaking of her phone, the request came through for us to get her records."

"They just arrived fifteen minutes ago," Luca supplied, looking up from his laptop to glance at both of them. "In the half hour before Kate tried to speak to Willie Jay, she got two phone calls. One from Brad and the other from Hamlin."

Joelle huffed. "Obviously, we'll be doing a lot of interviews today."

"They're already set up," Duncan assured her. "As soon as you're done eating, we can head to the hospital and knock out the one with Kate. Then, I can have an actual breakfast delivered for you from the diner while we wait for first Brad and then Hamlin to come in."

Duncan expected they'd have lawyers with them and would deny everything. But the pieces were there, and maybe, just maybe, those pieces would fit so one of them or Kate could be arrested today.

"I do have one bit of good news," Joelle said. "I had a text conversation with Bree before I got in the shower, and I convinced her not to come home right now."

Good. That was one less person who might get caught up in this messy investigation.

"I can eat my apple on the way to the hospital," Joelle insisted. "I'm eager to hear what Kate has to say."

So was he, but Duncan took a moment to make sure Joelle was up to this. One glance at her and he knew she was. He couldn't say she looked rested, but she was clearly raring to go. So, that's what he did.

With Luca grabbing his laptop, Duncan headed to the window—again—to make sure there wasn't anyone lurking around. When he didn't see anyone, they went to the cruiser and started the cautious drive to the hospital. Only a couple of minutes. But if the missing gunman and his boss had realized Duncan and Joelle had spent the night at his place, then they might have set some kind of booby trap on the road.

Luca and Joelle no doubt expected the worst, too, because they kept watch. Joelle did the entire five-minute drive with her hand over the butt of her weapon. Thankfully, though, they made it to their destination without anyone trying to kill them.

Despite the early hour, there were already several cars in the parking lot, but Luca parked close enough to the door that Joelle only had a short distance out in the open before she hurried in through the ER doors. Duncan was right there with her, and he did a sweeping check of the ER. No one suspicious.

With Luca staying close behind them, Joelle and Duncan made their way to Kate's door, and Duncan was pleased when he saw Clyde Granger standing guard. Clyde was in his sixties now and a retired deputy, but Duncan knew the man was still plenty sharp.

"She's whining," Clyde said, his tone indicating this wasn't the first time. "She won't leave without police protection."

"So Dr. Benton told me," Duncan verified. "I'll consider it." He was stretched thin with manpower and was surprised that Kate hadn't just hired private security. The woman certainly had enough money to do that.

Luca stayed in the hall with Clyde when they reached the room. Kate immediately sat up in bed, and she had her phone gripped as if ready to call 911. She audibly released her breath when she saw it was Joelle and Duncan.

"Dr. Benton said he's releasing me this morning," she said like a protest.

Duncan nodded. "He said you believed you were in danger."

"I am," Kate was quick to verify. She glanced away, then. "Maybe in danger from my own son. Did you arrest him?"

"I'm questioning him," Duncan supplied, and he considered that the end to him answering the woman's questions. He hadn't come here for that. "Tell me why you called the sheriff's office last night and asked to speak to a prisoner we had in custody."

Kate didn't look surprised. Probably because she would have known all calls would be logged. Especially calls made to a criminal like Willie Jay.

"That PI, Al Hamlin, phoned me," Kate snarled with plenty of venom in her voice now. "He told me you'd arrested a man named Willie Jay Prescott, and that the man was going to tell you and the deputies that I had been the one who arranged to kidnap the dispatcher and Deputy McCullough."

"Did you?" Duncan demanded.

"No." That came out as a howl of outrage, followed by a groan and a lot of head shaking. "Of course not. I wouldn't do something like that."

The jury was still out on that, but Duncan tried a different angle. "Tell me about Arlo Dennison."

No howl of outrage this time, but there was plenty of surprise. "Why do you want to know about him?"

Duncan gave her a hard look to let her know she would be answering questions, not him.

Kate's mouth tightened. "Arlo managed one of my gyms. And I know what you're going to say," she continued when Duncan's look hardened even more. "That PI told you he talked with Arlo when he and his girlfriend were giving up their baby for adoption."

"He did." And Duncan made a circling motion with his finger for her to continue.

She obeyed, after she huffed. "I was very busy with work when all of that was going on, but a friend of a friend wanted to adopt a baby. So, when I got word of Hamlin and his girlfriend, I made the initial contact. Arlo followed up with them. But you should know that I had no idea Hamlin and his girlfriend wanted money for the baby. They were convicted, you know."

"And you and Arlo were questioned," Duncan reminded her. Ruston had come across that tidbit and passed it along.

"We were," she admitted, "but nothing came of it because there was nothing to find. I was trying to do this friend of a friend a favor, and I got caught up in the middle of an ugly mess. Now Hamlin thinks I took his sister and am running some kind of baby-selling business. I can assure you, I'm not."

Kate looked ready to add more to that protest, but the

sound of some loud talking in the hall stopped her. "Brad," she muttered when she obviously recognized one of those voices.

Duncan knew the other voice was Clyde's, and the deputy was clearly in an argument with Kate's son.

"I want to see my mother now," Brad demanded.

His first thought was to send Brad on his way to the sheriff's office so he could wait for the interview. But then Duncan figured it would be interesting to see how mother and son reacted to each other, especially since there were four deputies ready to intercede if Brad did try to go after Kate. Or vice versa.

Throwing open the door, Duncan silenced Brad with one of the glares he'd been doling out to Kate for the past five minutes or so. Brad froze for a moment, but then moved darn fast when Duncan motioned for him to come inside.

"I don't want him here," Kate snapped.

Duncan ignored her, but he also blocked Brad when he attempted to charge closer to Kate. "Since you clearly have something to say to your mother, say it," Duncan invited.

Brad had another momentary freeze before he speared his mother's gaze with his. "You told Hamlin I hired gunmen to go after Deputy McCullough and the dispatcher."

Kate's shoulders went stiff. "I most certainly did not." She muttered some profanity. "And I'm tired of being accused of things I didn't do," she added to Duncan.

"Hamlin said he called you and that you said I should be arrested before I tried to kill you," Brad insisted.

Kate huffed. "No." She stretched out that word. "Hamlin's the one who pointed the finger at you, and he didn't say anything to me about you trying to kill me. Hamlin, however, did warn me about that prisoner, Willie Jay Prescott. Hamlin claimed you hired him."

Silence fell over the room while they all took a moment to process that. Duncan didn't need a moment, though, since he'd already come to a conclusion.

"Hamlin could be trying to stir up trouble between you two," Duncan pointed out. "More trouble," he amended, "since it's obvious that things aren't lovey-dovey."

"They aren't," Kate muttered, and her face tightened. Duncan figured it had occurred to her that he was right, that Hamlin had called both Kate and Brad to get them at each other's throats.

And it had worked.

It made Duncan wonder if Hamlin had done that with the hopes it would get Kate to say something to incriminate herself in the illegal baby sales. Or if Brad would be the one doing the self-incriminating. If so, Hamlin could have wanted that to cover up his own guilt. In fact, all the attacks and Molly's kidnapping could be to set up either Brad or Kate so Hamlin would escape scrutiny for his pregnant sister's disappearance.

"My lawyer is on his way to Saddle Ridge," Brad muttered a moment later. "I'll talk to him about suing Hamlin for slander."

Duncan didn't tell Brad that would be a long shot and turn into a "he said, she said." Added to that, Kate probably wouldn't want all of this to be rehashed in public, which it would be if there was a lawsuit.

Brad continued to stare at Kate while his jaw muscles tightened. "Look me in the eyes, Mother, and tell me you had nothing to do with Shanda being murdered."

The anger on Kate's face had cooled a bit, but that caused it to heat up again. "No, I did not, and I'm insulted you even asked."

"I have to ask," Brad fired back, "because you hated her."

Kate opened her mouth, and must have rethought what she was about to say. "Yes, I hated her because of the person you became once you got involved with her," she finally said, her voice surprisingly calm. "You changed after Shanda lost that baby. You became obsessed with payback."

"Obsessed with getting my family back," he quickly replied. "I wanted Shanda and a baby."

"You wanted revenge," Kate spelled out.

Brad glared at her. But he didn't disagree. However, Brad did turn and head out the door. It was still open since Luca and Clyde had both been keeping a close eye on the situation.

Duncan went after Brad so he could remind the man about the interview, but when he went into the hall, he saw that Brad was practically charging toward someone.

Hamlin.

The PI was coming straight up the hall, and the men rammed into each other. That caused them to collide with a nurse carrying a tray of meds, all of which went flying.

So did the fists.

Brad managed to punch Hamlin in the face before Duncan could get to him. Hamlin retaliated, throwing his own punch, and the hall was suddenly filled with profanity-laced tirades and the sounds of the struggle. The nurse was trapped beneath the men.

Duncan reached into the heap and pulled out the nurse, sliding her toward Joelle who had moved closer to help. Once Joelle had the nurse out of the way, Duncan went after Brad next and hauled him out of the fray by the collar of his shirt. Clyde and Luca took hold of Hamlin, who came off the floor ready to run at Brad again.

"You lying SOB," Brad yelled, and he added plenty more profanity to go along with that. Hamlin was doing the same.

Duncan glanced at Joelle who was moving the nurse back toward the nurses' station. "Call for two deputies," Duncan instructed Joelle. "I want both Brad and Hamlin taken to holding cells."

That would keep both men off the streets at least until Duncan had a chance to interview them. It was possible, likely even, that Brad and Hamlin would be filing assault charges against each other. But he'd deal with all of that later. For now, Duncan needed to establish some calm and control since a crowd had gathered to see what the ruckus was all about. There were at least a dozen medical folks and patients gawking at the two men being restrained and the now-crying nurse.

"I can get this one to the cruiser now," Luca offered, keeping a firm grip on Hamlin. "Once he's in holding, I can come back for Joelle and you."

"Do that," Duncan agreed. As long as Brad and Hamlin were around each other, there'd be the possibility of another altercation.

Luca immediately got a still-cursing Hamlin moving toward the ER doors, and when Brad tried to go after the PI, Duncan had had enough. He pulled out some plastic cuffs from his pocket and restrained Brad.

"Go back and stay with Kate," Duncan told Clyde. "I'll look for a place to stash Brad until the other deputies arrive." Duncan also wanted to check on the nurse. She didn't appear to be injured, but she had taken a hard fall.

Duncan got Brad moving toward Joelle and the nurse, but he'd only made it a couple of steps before Clyde called out to him. Duncan turned to see Clyde standing in front of Kate's still open door.

"The room's empty, Sheriff," Clyde said. "Kate's gone."

JOELLE READ THE text from Woodrow to let her know that Ronnie and he had Brad out of the hospital and in their cruiser. Thankfully, she'd already gotten a text from Luca to let them know he'd arrived safely with Hamlin, and that the PI was now in a holding cell where he'd wait until Duncan and she could get back to the sheriff's office.

Whenever that would be.

There was a full-scale search going on for Kate not only in the hospital but also the grounds. Since Duncan hadn't wanted Joelle out of his sight, they had taken the patients wing with the hopes that a frightened Kate had ducked into one of them to avoid another confrontation with her son.

So far, nothing.

And that's what Clyde and some of the orderlies were reporting as they searched the grounds. Kate had seemingly vanished, and Joelle knew that couldn't be a good thing.

In the chaos of the fight, it was possible someone had sneaked in and taken Kate. There was a good argument to be made for that since Kate's phone had been left on the bed. If the woman had fled of her own accord, she likely would have taken that. Then again, she might have left it behind since the phone could be used to pinpoint her whereabouts.

If so, Kate might have left out of fear of her own arrest.

Duncan huffed when they cleared another room and there was still no sign of Kate. At least this particular room hadn't had a patient. Some of the others had been occupied, and it had to be unsettling to have two cops show up and conduct a search. Joelle had doled out a lot of apologies. Not just to the patients but the nurse who'd been shaken up in the brawl. Thankfully, the woman hadn't been hurt other than some bruising and frayed nerves.

"Three more to go," Duncan muttered when they went

back into the hall. "And supposedly none is occupied." He'd likely gotten that info from one of the nurses since Duncan's phone had been dinging every few minutes with texts.

As they'd done with the other rooms, Duncan kept his gun ready while he eased open a door and peered inside. Once he'd done the initial check of the main part of the room, Joelle stepped in to cover him so he could have a look in the bathroom.

"Empty," he said, and he stopped to read another text. "The hospital security guard is searching the roof to see if Kate went up there."

Joelle figured if the woman was going to run, it wouldn't be to the roof where she would essentially end up trapped since there was only one set of stairs leading to it. Still, Kate might not be thinking straight.

Duncan and she went back into the hall, which had thankfully been cleared of any gawkers, and they made their way to the next room. This one was easier than some of the others since the bathroom door was wide open, so all they had to do was a cursory sweep before moving on to the final room. Once they checked it, they'd be able to head to the sheriff's office where they could question Brad and Hamlin while the search for Kate continued.

They came to a quick stop outside the final room when there was a thumping sound just on the other side of the door. Duncan glanced back at her, a silent warning for her to use extra caution. She would. Because even if it was Kate in there, it didn't mean the woman wouldn't attack them. Maybe out of fear.

Maybe, though, because Kate was the killer.

Duncan motioned for Joelle to stand back, and he eased open the door. Unlike the other rooms, this one was pitch-dark, probably because someone had lowered the blinds.

Joelle barely managed a glance inside when she heard another sound. One that she instantly recognized.

A stun gun.

"Duncan," she managed to call out.

But it was too late.

The gloved hand that snaked out of the darkness jammed the stun gun against Duncan's throat. He staggered back, and Joelle reached for him, trying to break his fall, but she didn't get to him in time. Duncan dropped like a stone.

Oh, God.

"Duncan," she shouted.

Joelle automatically drew her gun. But it was too late for that, too. A bulky man wearing orderly scrubs and a ski mask charged right at her, pushing her back against the wall. In the same motion, he tried to knock the gun from her hand. She held on, twisting her body to try and get away from him so she'd have a clean shot. No chance of that since this thug might deflect the gun, and the bullet could hit Duncan.

"Officer down," she yelled, hoping that someone would hear her and come running.

The thug must have thought that was a possibility, too, because he clamped his hand on hers and her gun and started muscling her toward the exit. He was not only tall but strong. A lot stronger than she was, but Joelle knew she had to fight him.

For her baby's sake.

For Duncan's.

This goon might turn and shoot Duncan before he made that final push to get her out of the building. Kidnapping her. Just as Willie Jay had tried. And the other two dead gunmen.

Joelle didn't want to mentally play out what would happen to her if he did manage to get her outside and into a vehicle. Instead, she focused on the baby and Duncan and tried not to let the terror take over.

She stomped as hard as she could on the goon's foot, and while it slowed him down and made him curse her, it didn't stop him. So Joelle twisted around and rammed her elbow into his gut. That worked better than the foot stomp because he staggered back a step, his back smacking against the wall. He still managed to keep his beefy grip on her gun.

From the corner of her eye, Joelle saw Duncan struggling to move, and he was lifting his gun. She had no idea if he had the motor control yet to pull the trigger, and like her, he didn't have anything close to a clean shot.

The goon pushed himself away from the wall, throwing himself at her and off-balancing her. Joelle had no choice but to protect her stomach, and she did that by bending forward. Not an easy task because of the baby bump, but she used her upper torso to protect her child.

Her attacker cursed her, and as Willie Jay had done, he latched onto her hair. The pain shot through her. With his other hand on her gun, he probably hoped to use that leverage and the pain to force her to move.

That failed, thank heavens.

Joelle got another slam of adrenaline. Another punch of the fight mode, and she used that strength and her training to twist his hand. And her gun. Until she had it aimed at his right leg.

She fired.

He yelled, the sound echoing along with the blast of the shot. Staggering, he let go of her hair, and the maneuver allowed her to take aim again. At his left leg. The bullet slammed into him and caused him to drop to his knees.

Joelle heard the sound of running footsteps and Slater

calling out to her. Help would be here soon. But she didn't take her attention off the goon. She couldn't see his face, but she figured it had to be twisted in pain.

"Move and I'll put another bullet in you," she warned him, wrenching her hand from his grip.

The goon didn't listen. He moved, reaching out so fast that it was just a blur of motion. But before Joelle could pull the trigger, someone else did.

Duncan.

He was still on the floor, but he'd lifted his head and shooting hand enough to deliver the fatal shot. Her attacker slumped forward. *Dead.*

Chapter Thirteen

Duncan paced while he waited on hold with Slater. Paced and kept his eye on Joelle who was now seated at his kitchen table.

Since she'd been covered with their attacker's blood, he'd brought her here to his place instead of the sheriff's office so she could shower. That was after she'd had yet another exam to make sure both she and the baby were all right.

They were. By some miracle, they were.

So was he since he'd also needed to be checked to make sure the stun gun hadn't done any permanent damage. It hadn't.

Duncan figured he'd be saying a lot of thanks and prayers for that. After he'd put an end to the danger so Joelle could make it through a blasted day without someone trying to kidnap her again. Because that's what had happened. Another attempted kidnapping. If the masked thug had wanted her dead, he would have shot her the moment Duncan opened the door of that hospital room.

Even though she hadn't been shot or hurt beyond a few minor scrapes and bruises, it still twisted away at him that she'd come so close to being taken. He should have put more precautions in place to prevent that. And he would. He couldn't continue to put her in harm's way when so much was at stake.

That's why he'd brought Luca with him, and like before, the deputy was in Duncan's home office doing reports of this latest incident. *Incident*, he silently repeated, the anger rising in him again. A sterile word for something that damn sure hadn't been sterile. Joelle and he had been attacked, and Duncan had been forced to kill the SOB. He'd add more thanks and prayers for having regained enough feeling in his shooting hand to manage that. If not, Joelle would have had to do it, and Duncan didn't want her having to deal with that on top of everything else.

And *everything else* was huge.

She'd been attacked three times now, and while Molly thankfully hadn't been this time around, the dispatcher was shaken to the core. So much so that she'd asked Duncan to have not one but two reserve deputies stay with her. Duncan had complied, pulling the two off the search for Kate.

Kate was another investigative thorn in his side right now. There was no sign of her, and worse, she could have been the one who'd hired that thug to come after Joelle and him in the hospital. If Duncan hadn't allowed himself to get distracted by Brad and Hamlin's fight, then he might have seen the woman sneaking out.

Or being taken.

"Stop beating yourself up," Joelle muttered.

She was watching him and sipping some milk that Slater had had delivered, and she looked so small in the loaner clothes she'd gotten from the sheriff's office. Loose gray jogging pants and a black tee that was a couple sizes too big for her.

"I deserve to be beaten up," he was quick to remind her. "I should have brought you to the sheriff's office before I ever started searching for Kate."

Joelle lifted her shoulder, sighed and stood, going to

the fridge to refill her glass of milk. That meant walking right by him, and she brushed her arm against his. Probably not by accident. He took out the *probably* when he looked at her.

"Stop beating yourself up," she repeated. "I'm a cop, and I could have made the decision to go to the sheriff's office when Luca was transporting Hamlin. If I'd done that, then who's to say this kidnapper wouldn't have come after me in the cruiser. Willie Jay did."

He had to fight back the horrific images of that attempt and this one. There had been enough bad for a lifetime, and it wasn't over. It wouldn't be over until he had the culprit behind bars.

She reached up and touched her fingers to his forehead. Duncan didn't exactly recoil, but the touch hurt a little. When he'd fallen after being stunned, his head had smacked on the floor, and the gash had needed a couple of stitches. He'd gotten those in the ER while the doctor had been examining Joelle and the baby.

There was finally a crackle of sound on the other end of the phone, and a moment later, Duncan heard Slater's voice. He went ahead and put the call on speaker since this was an update Joelle would want to hear.

"The dead guy is Arlo Dennison," Slater provided.

Hell. That circled right back to Kate since the man had been one of her employees. It was possible Arlo had still been an employee, just in a different capacity as a hired gun.

"Four dead men," Slater emphasized. "That could mean whoever hired them has run out of muscle."

Maybe. But Duncan knew it was just as likely that Kate, Brad or Hamlin had found yet someone else to do their dirty work.

"Still no sign of Kate," Slater went on. "The Texas Rangers you requested arrived, and they're coordinating the search."

Good. Duncan figured if the woman could be found, the Rangers were his best shot at making that happen. Especially since Kate could be anywhere right now. She hadn't taken her phone with her, but she could have arranged for someone to meet her in the parking lot and take her to heavens knew where.

"Luca just filed yours and Joelle's statements on the attack at the hospital," Slater added a moment later.

No surprise there. Luca had been the one to take those statements shortly after they'd come to his place. Both Joelle's and Duncan's primary weapons and clothes had also been taken into evidence. All standard procedure. So was counseling, but that was going to have to wait.

"Any updates on Brad and Hamlin?" Duncan said to Slater.

Duncan already knew both men had made bail and the interviews had been rescheduled for late afternoon. Not with Joelle and him doing them, either. Going with standard procedure again, neither of them would be doing interviews and such until there'd been a review of how they'd handled Arlo's attack.

"Nothing new," Slater said. "Well, nothing other than both men's lawyers are clamoring about their clients being innocent and harassed by the cops. Same ol', same ol'," he muttered. Then, paused. "How's Joelle? And, yes, I'm asking you, Duncan, because my sister might not tell me the truth."

"I'm okay," she insisted. "Okay-ish," Joelle amended when Slater huffed and Duncan gave her a flat stare. "You should be asking about Duncan. He's the one beating himself up over what happened. I'm not. We did what we had to do to stay alive and keep our baby safe."

Duncan continued to study her, to see if she'd said that to ease her brother's mind. And his. But Joelle seemed to have processed this and just might actually be okay-ish.

"I'll keep an eye on Joelle," Duncan told Slater, not only because it was true but because he also wanted to relieve Slater's worries. It would relieve Duncan's worries about her, too.

He ended the call, and when he went to put his phone away, he saw the blood smears on the back of his hand. His own blood from the cut on his head. It was a reminder that unlike Joelle, he hadn't showered.

"Shower," he muttered when he saw that her attention, too, had landed on the blood, and Duncan decided it was time to remedy that.

Time to remedy something else, too.

Duncan pulled Joelle to him and kissed her. Really kissed her. Yeah, it was a stupid thing to do, but it was necessary. He needed to have her close, this close, if only for a moment or two.

He didn't deepen the kiss. Didn't move them body to body, even though a certain part of him immediately started urging him to do just that. Duncan just kept the kiss gentle and hopefully comforting. Because he was damn sure they both needed that right now.

When he finally eased back, he stared down into her eyes and braced himself for her to warn him they were playing with fire. Which they were. But she simply smiled.

"Shower," she muttered. "Then, we can...talk."

That idiot part of him got all excited that sex might happen. It didn't matter that it would be a bad idea.

At least, it probably would be.

Joelle likely wasn't thinking straight and didn't need to land in bed with him. But her mention of *talk* had nixed the bed thing, and unlike sex, that was probably a good thing. She no doubt had things she needed to say about the attack. Maybe things about all this kissing they'd been doing.

Duncan headed to his bedroom for that shower, but he stopped by the office to check on Luca. He was still typing up reports. "Statements from the people interviewed at the hospital," Luca muttered without taking his attention off the screen.

A necessary pain in the butt. And something might be in those statements they could use. It was a serious long shot, though.

Duncan was thankful that Joelle followed him to his bedroom. Not because of the possibility of that sex happening, but because he didn't want her too far away from him. The security system was on, and two of Slater's ranch hands were outside in a truck, watching the place—something they'd been doing since he and Joelle had arrived from the hospital. A lot of avenues had been covered, but Duncan still wanted Joelle close so he'd be able to get to her fast if there was another attack.

Joelle sat on the foot of his bed while he headed to the shower. He didn't close the bathroom door between them. Another precaution, in case she called out to him for help. He hoped like hell there wouldn't be any such need for that.

Duncan turned on the shower, and stripped while he waiting for the water to reach the right temperature. The moment it was warm enough, he stepped in so he could do this fast and minimize the time Joelle was out of his sight. He had barely gotten started on it, though, when the shower door opened, and Joelle was standing there.

Joelle, who slid her gaze down the entire length of his body.

Duncan's gaze did some sliding as well. Looking at every

inch of her. Man, she was beautiful. Always had been. But the baby bump actually added to that beauty.

He went hard as stone.

"I haven't been with anyone else but you since, well, in a very long time," she said.

It took him a moment to realize why she'd volunteered that. Then, he spotted the condom that she had likely taken from the drawer of his nightstand. It was a reminder they'd used one five months ago, and she'd still gotten pregnant.

"I haven't been with anyone else, either, in a long time," he told her and could have added that she was the only woman he wanted.

"So, not necessary," she muttered, tossing the condom onto the vanity.

Without taking her attention off him, she pulled off the loose clothes, tossing them on the floor next to his.

"I'll be careful," she said when he glanced down at the wet tiled floor. "Maybe you can hold on tight to me to make sure we don't slip."

And she stepped inside under the spray of warm water. In the same motion, she looped her arm around his neck and pulled him to her.

She kissed him.

Hard, hungry and long. This was no kiss of comfort, and yet it accomplished just that. Comfort. Then, a whole mountain of heat. She kissed and kissed until the nightmarish images just slid away.

"The bathroom door is locked," she muttered. "Our phones are right on the vanity where we'll be able to hear them. And we aren't going to think about this," she tacked onto that.

Good. Because Duncan didn't want to think. He just wanted Joelle, and he wanted her now. Apparently, she was on the same page because she added some clever touching to the deep kiss. She slid her hand between their naked bodies. Down his chest. To his stomach. Then, over his erection.

If Duncan had actually wanted to do any thinking, that would have put an end to it. The only thing on his mind right now was taking Joelle.

Joelle got that taking started by hooking her arms around his neck and pulling herself up. He gladly helped with that by putting his arm underneath her bottom and lifting her until they were facing each other.

The kiss continued, raging on, cranking up the heat even more. But that heat was a drop in the bucket compared to Joelle's wet breasts sliding against his chest and with their centers pressed right against each other.

Duncan had to fight the urge just to push into her, to give both their bodies what they were demanding. But he purposely slowed so he could savor this. He eased back on the urgency of the kiss, and he kept his touch light as he cupped her breasts and flicked his thumb over her nipple.

She gave an aroused moan, and her head lolled to the side, exposing her throat. Duncan took advantage of that and slid both his mouth and tongue down her neck. Pleasuring her. Pleasuring himself.

The angle was all wrong for him to kiss her breasts so he levered her up even more, using the shower wall to stop them from falling. Once he had her high enough, he took one of her nipples into his mouth.

This time her moan was a whole lot louder, and the kiss kicked up the urgency again. She worked her way back down, aligning their centers again, notching up Duncan's own urgency when she slid herself against him.

No way could he hold off after that so he anchored her

again by holding her bottom while he pushed into her. He got an instant slam of sensations. Pleasure. So much pleasure. But more. This was right. This was exactly what he'd been waiting for these past five months. Hell, longer. Since he'd wanted Joelle for as long as he could remember.

It was a balancing act to stay on his feet, but Duncan adjusted his position, and he started the slow deep strokes inside her. All thoughts of, well, pretty much everything vanished. Everything except this. The right here, right now. Everything except Joelle.

The need clawed its way through him, driving him to move faster. Pushing him to give Joelle both the pleasure and the release from this intense heat. It happened, and it didn't take long. Not with their bodies starved for each other. Duncan only needed a few of those strokes when he felt her muscles clamp around him. When he felt the climax ripple through her.

"Duncan," she muttered, dropping her head onto his shoulder.

And that was all he needed to push him right over the edge. Duncan held Joelle close and found his own release.

Chapter Fourteen

Joelle's entire body felt slack. Sated. Incredible. But she also knew without a doubt that she wouldn't be able to stand on what she was sure would be wobbly legs.

Duncan took care of that.

Just as he'd taken care of her with that sexual release.

He turned off the shower, scooped her up in his arms and stepped with her onto the rug. He didn't stop there, either, but rather sat her on the vanity while he pulled a huge towel around her. Since he proceeded to dry her off, that meant she got an amazing view of his completely naked wet body.

Mercy, she wanted him all over again.

This had been the problem with them for years. The heat. The need. And she'd thought that once they finally ended up in bed five months ago, the need would lessen some. It hadn't. And later, she was going to consider why that was. Consider, too, if it would ever go away.

Judging from the way her body was humming, the answer to that was no.

After he dried her off, he kissed her again. One of those scorching, heart-melting post-sex kisses that held promises of more to come. Too bad her body was absolutely onboard for that. Her mind, though, was reminding her to hold back, to guard her heart. And to put up those barriers again.

Joelle didn't do any of that.

She kissed him right back in the full-throttle mode. It lasted some very long moments, and when she eased back, she saw the fresh heat in those amazing eyes of his. The corner of his mouth lifted, flashing her a smile that also fell into the amazing category.

Of course, the smile didn't last. It faded by degrees, but at least she'd gotten to enjoy it for a bit.

"I'm guessing we'll have that talk now," he muttered, not sounding the least bit enthusiastic about that.

Neither was she, but Joelle thought they should spell out that this could be temporary. That this was "no strings attached" sex. Because she didn't want Duncan to feel this had to be the start of some grand commitment. He'd already committed to the baby, both offering child support and shared custody, and that was enough.

Had to be enough.

Joelle wasn't exactly sure what her feelings were for him… She stopped, mentally regrouped. All right, she was sure. She cared deeply for Duncan. Was perhaps leaning toward being in love with him. But this was so not the right time to delve into all of that.

"Let's put the talk on hold," she suggested. "Instead, let's go over the reports Luca's done, and I'll see if he needs help with any others."

Of course, Joelle had offered to help Luca when they'd arrived at Duncan's, and he'd declined, telling her to get some rest. Sex had been an incredible substitute for rest, and now she wanted to dive back into the investigation.

Duncan didn't seem convinced. He frowned. She wasn't sure if that was because he did, indeed, want to talk. Or maybe he wanted to keep kissing her and go for round two of sex. That was tempting. Mercy, was it.

"The sooner we make an arrest, the sooner the baby will be safe," she said, knowing Duncan was already well aware of that.

However, it seemed to be the exact nudge he needed to move away from her and start drying off. He did mutter some profanity, though, under his breath that had her smiling again.

Joelle started to get dressed, and despite the reminder she'd just given him, she didn't ignore the peep show going on right in front of her. Duncan was hot, but he was even hotter when he was naked.

He pulled on his boxers, his gaze meeting hers, and she saw the heat that was still there. She felt the tug deep within her body. Not sexual. Well, not totally. This was something different. Something just as strong. And it had her going back to falling in love with him. She probably would have had a mental debate with herself about that had her phone not rang.

She got a jolt when she looked at the screen and saw *Unknown Caller*, and part of her realized she'd been waiting for another would-be kidnapper to get in touch with her. Yes, four hired guns were dead, but Joelle was pretty sure their boss was still out there somewhere.

Out there and had possibly already hired new thugs to come after her.

Duncan became all cop, and he hit the recorder on his phone a split second before he nodded for her to take the call. She did, expecting to hear some muffled threatening voice of a stranger.

She didn't.

"Joelle?" the woman asked.

She nearly dropped the phone. "It's my mother," she said, the words rushing out with her breath. She looked at

Duncan to see if he'd recognized it as well. He did, and he looked just as stunned as she was.

"Mom," Joelle finally managed. "Where are you? How are you?" And she had so many other questions she wanted to add to that.

For five months, she'd been terrified for her mother. Not only for her mom's safety since Joelle considered that she, too, might be dead. But there had also been the worry that Sandra McCullough had somehow participated in her husband's murder. Or was on the run because of something she'd learned or witnessed.

"Joelle," her mom repeated, but she didn't launch right into answering those questions. "I need help."

The static crackled across the phone connection, but Joelle still heard that loud and clear. "Where are you?" she repeated. "What's wrong?"

Again, there wasn't a quick answer, and the static increased. There was also the sound of a revving car engine.

"I'm at the ranch," her mother finally said. "Please, Joelle, please, come and get me before it's too late."

JOELLE FELT AS if she'd had way too much caffeine and her mind was whirling from it. However, the jumble of thoughts wasn't from any coffee but rather from hearing her mother's voice.

Slater was hearing it now, too.

Her brother and Carmen had arrived within minutes after Joelle had phoned him to let him know about the call, and now Slater was standing in Duncan's living room, listening to the recording. It wasn't the first time Slater had played it, either. This was his third, and he seemed just as shell-shocked as she had been.

Still was.

"That's Mom's voice," she muttered to Slater. That was a repeat as well.

Her brother made a soft sound of agreement, and he looked up as if yanking himself out of a trance. "Yeah. But you know this is some kind of a trap."

"She knows," Duncan was quick to say.

Joelle did, indeed, and that's what had prevented her from bolting out of Duncan's house, jumping into the cruiser and driving straight to her family's ranch. Because this could all be a ploy to draw her out into the open like that. But there was a flipside to this.

Her mother could be in grave danger.

Could be.

And that was the sticking point here. Slater obviously knew something about that *could be* because he played the recording once more. Duncan and she had done the same thing when they'd waited for Slater to arrive.

"The call was almost certainly made from a burner," Slater pointed out, and Joelle made a sound of agreement. That was being checked as they spoke. Techs were also repeatedly trying to call the number with the hopes that someone would answer. So far, nothing.

"Mom never answered any of your questions," her brother added a moment later.

Joelle nodded. "And there's the static. A lot of it," she emphasized. "It seems to be coming from maybe a TV station or radio that's offline. It's too steady for the intermittent kind of static you'd get from a bad phone connection."

Slater nodded as well, and he shifted his attention to Duncan. "So, the fact that we're not charging over to the ranch right now tells me you don't believe my mother is actually in danger."

"I wish I knew for sure," Duncan said, drawing in a long

breath. "It is Sandra's voice," he verified. "But it could have been spliced together from old recordings. Maybe interviews taken from the internet."

Her mother had certainly done some of those since she'd often campaigned for bond issues to better fund the schools and libraries. Joelle couldn't recall a specific speech or such that could have been used to piece together what she'd heard, but it was possible. There was a huge *but*, though, in all of this.

"If the killer actually has her…" Joelle started, but then she couldn't force out the rest of it. Not aloud, anyway. But inside her head, the possibility was flashing bright and nonstop.

Her mother could be murdered.

She could be being held right now. Could be hurt. And she could need their help. In fact, it was possible her father's killer had taken her mother five months ago and had been holding her all this time, planning to use her to punish Joelle for whatever the killer believed she needed to be punished for. Maybe Brad for what'd happened to Shanda. Maybe Kate because her father had been on her trail for the illegal baby sales. Or Hamlin who wanted revenge for his arrest as a juvenile.

Duncan was well aware of that, too, and that's why he'd spent the past fifteen minutes assembling a team. Or rather two of them. And even though Duncan hadn't spelled it out yet, Joelle was pretty sure she knew what he was planning.

"You'll stay here," Duncan said, his gaze spearing hers. "I would take you to the sheriff's office, but this SOB could be hoping for that. To attack us along the road and try to take you."

Joelle had already considered that as well. It was the very definition of a rock and a hard place. If she went anywhere, she was a target. Ditto for if she stayed put. Duncan couldn't stop that, but he could maybe stop her mother from being killed if she was being held at the ranch.

"Luca and Carmen will stay here with you," Duncan went on. "And the two armed ranch hands will continue to guard the grounds. They'll block the driveway to prevent anyone from using a vehicle to get to the house. Stay inside and keep the security system on."

She recalled him saying all the windows and doors were rigged so if someone did attempt to break in, they'd at least get a warning. Then, whoever tried to get inside would be facing three cops.

"Slater and I will go to the ranch," Duncan continued a moment later.

But Joelle immediately interrupted him. "And you'll have extra backup with you," she insisted. "As we learned with Molly, there are plenty of places for someone to lie in wait."

Duncan didn't argue. "Ronnie and Woodrow are already on the way to the ranch. They'll hang back and use binoculars and infrared to try and spot any threats. Try and spot your mother, too, if she's actually there." He checked the time. "The plan is to make this as quick as possible."

His gaze lingered on Joelle's for a couple of moments, and she nodded. Not because she liked the idea but because there wasn't another option. The ranch had to be checked, and Duncan was the sheriff.

He went to her, and while he didn't kiss her, not with other cops watching, Duncan took her hand and gave it a gentle squeeze. "It's only a trap if we aren't ready for it, and we are," he whispered to her. "We'll take every possible precaution, and I want you to do the same."

She nodded again. "Come back to me in one piece," she muttered.

Duncan looked as if he wanted to groan at that. Because it seemed to be the start of some grand confession about her feelings for him. About how important he was to her.

Which he was.

But no way did she want to send him off with that kind of distraction running through his mind.

"Stay safe," she added, using her cop's voice, and Joelle purposely turned away from him and faced Luca. "I can help you type up the witness statements from the hospital."

That would give her something to focus on. Or rather something to try to focus on. Joelle didn't know how long this would take Duncan and the others, but she would be on pins and needles the entire time.

"I'll reset the security system with my phone once we're out," Duncan relayed to her as Slater and he went to the door. Both Duncan and her brother gave her one last look before they headed out. One last stomach-twisting look.

Joelle stayed put, listening, and she heard the sound of the cruiser ignition. Heard, too, when Slater and Duncan drove away.

And the waiting began.

"Luca, I can do some reports as well," Carmen said, drawing Joelle's attention back to the other deputies. "So email me the notes of the ones you want me to do," she added as she took out her laptop.

Carmen didn't sit in the kitchen though but rather moved to the front window. No doubt so she could keep watch.

Since the keeping watch was a good idea, Joelle tipped her head to the hall. "Duncan's bedroom has a good view of the backyard. I can work from there. And yes, I'll stay back from the windows."

Luca didn't make a sound of agreement until she added that last part. "The office has a view of the east side of the property, and since that side doesn't face any of Duncan's neighbors, I can keep an eye on things from there. I'll email you both some of the statement notes," he added, heading to the office.

Joelle took her laptop and went into Duncan's bedroom. Of course, it was a reminder that less than an hour ago they'd had shower sex. *Amazing shower sex.* But since that brought on images of Duncan, the worry came with it, and she said a flurry of quick prayers that Duncan, her brother, Woodrow and Ronnie would come out of this unscathed.

Her mother, too.

Part of her wanted to hope her mother was there at the ranch. Because if she was, then it meant she probably hadn't voluntarily left her family. But if that was the case, then it was unbearable to think of the hell her mother had gone through all these months.

Since that kind of thinking wasn't helping her already frayed nerves, Joelle got to work—away from the window, though, she did open the curtains enough for her to be able to see out. There was a small seating area in the corner of the bedroom, and Joelle turned the chair so it was facing the window. That would keep her in the shadows and hopefully out of the line of sight of any shooters.

While she booted up her computer, she glanced out in the backyard. Unlike her place, this area wasn't thick with trees. Just the opposite. There was a small barn and some white wood pasture fence. A shooter wouldn't be able to use the fence to hide or sneak up closer to the house.

But the barn was a different matter.

The door was closed, and if a determined shooter belly-crawled through the pasture, they could slip behind the barn and try to fire into the house. With that unsettling thought,

Joelle wasn't sure how much work she would get done, but she opened the file that Luca sent her, anyway.

There had apparently been thirty-one statements taken from patients, medical staff and anyone who happened to be in the parking lot at the time Arlo launched his attack and Kate went missing. Luca had sent Joelle six, nowhere near the one-third he should have given her. When she got through these, she would ask for more.

The statements were basically notes taken by the questioning officers, and they needed to be cleaned up and put in an official file that would then have to be verified and signed by those interviewers. Normally, cops did their own reports, but with so many aspects to the investigation, they all needed to chip in. Especially since she wasn't the one out there looking for Kate.

Joelle made it through the first one when she heard a soft thumping sound coming from the large walk-in closet/dressing area that was on the other side of the bathroom. The closet door was closed, and there wasn't a window in there that someone could use to break in.

She waited, her fingers poised on the keyboard while she continued to listen. Nothing.

And she was ready to dismiss it when she heard it again.

Joelle quietly set her laptop aside and got to her feet. She drew her weapon and inched to the closet door while also keeping watch of the window in the bedroom. It occurred to her that someone could be tossing something against the exterior wall to distract her so they could make sure no one was watching them if they sneaked up to the barn.

She stopped to send a text to Frankie Mendoza, one of Slater's ranch hands who was out front watching the road.

Do you see anyone on the right side of the house toward the back?

Joelle's heartbeat kicked up a few notches while she waited the couple of seconds it took him to answer. No one's there, Frankie replied.

That settled her down some, but Joelle remembered Duncan whispering to her about taking every possible precaution so she decided to get some help, especially since she was only a couple of feet away from the closet door. Even though it should have set off the security alarms, maybe someone had managed to get into the house.

"Luca?" she called out, keeping her voice calm and level. "Could you come here a second?" If it turned out to be nothing, then she would owe him an apology for interrupting him.

But it was something.

Before Joelle even heard Luca's footsteps, there were two loud thumps as if something heavy had fallen onto the floor of the closet. Her gaze whipped to the closet door as it flew open.

The two men were wearing ski masks, and they charged right at her.

Duncan's stomach knotted when he saw the McCullough ranch come into view on the horizon. Considering the godawful things that'd happened here, the place had an eerie feel to it. The approaching storm didn't help, either. The thick clouds were an angry-looking slate gray and shut out so much of the light that it looked more like twilight than daytime.

He stopped the cruiser at the end of the road and fired glances all around while Slater sent off a text to Woodrow. According to the two messages they'd already received from

Woodrow while Slater and he had been en route, Woodrow and Ronnie had arrived at the ranch about seven minutes earlier, and they had done an immediate check with the binoculars.

They'd seen no one.

So they'd driven slightly closer to accommodate the short range of the infrared, and they were about to scan for heat sources. Since the deputies should have had time to at least start that, Duncan needed an update.

"Nothing so far," Slater relayed when he got a response from Woodrow. "They're moving closer now that we're here."

Ahead of them, he saw the deputies' cruiser start inching toward the house. Duncan did the same, driving slightly faster than Woodrow since he wanted to be right there with them in case someone opened fire.

It'd been less than ten minutes since he'd left Joelle at his place. Ten minutes of constant worry and doubts. And now Duncan hoped he could do this search as fast as possible so he could get back to her. He had a bad feeling about this whole situation, but he didn't know if the feeling was because he and his deputies were in immediate danger.

Or if Joelle was.

Possibly all of them were.

So far, their attacker had used guns and the fire at Joelle's to attempt to kidnap her, but it was possible they had something much bigger in their arsenal now. Then again, they wouldn't need bigger if they had Joelle's mom. If Sandra was truly here, she would be a damn good bargaining tool. One no doubt designed to draw out Joelle.

Slater's phone dinged again. "Woodrow spotted a heat source in the center of the barn," he told Duncan as he read the text. "If it's a person, he or she is lying down."

Hell. Lying down because she could be tied up. Like proverbial bait.

"No other heat sources," Slater finished.

Of course, that didn't mean no one was around. If the hired guns or their boss figured infrared would be used, they could be staying just out of range.

"Tell Woodrow that I'm going to pull ahead of them," Duncan instructed Slater. "I'll have to knock down a fence, but I'll drive to the barn." Maybe even into the barn itself since the person wasn't near the entrance. That would keep Slater and him protected for a while longer.

While Slater dealt with sending the text, Duncan maneuvered around the other cruiser and drove through the yard. He accelerated when he got to the fence, and the reinforced cruiser bashed right through it. Wood went flying, some of it thumping against the cruiser, but Duncan didn't think there'd be any real damage to the vehicle. He'd owe the McCulloughs a fence, though.

"Heat source hasn't moved," Slater said, giving Duncan the latest update from Woodrow.

That added some weight to the possibility of the person being tied. Or maybe unconscious. Hell, perhaps even dead, because a body could continue to register as a heat source for minutes after dying.

Duncan was about to rev up to bash the front end of the cruiser into the barn door, but his phone rang. His heart went to his knees when he saw Luca's name on the screen.

"What's wrong?" Duncan immediately asked.

But he didn't get an immediate answer. And no answer at all from Luca. "It's me," Carmen said, and her trembling voice confirmed something was wrong.

"What happened?" Duncan snarled.

"Luca was hit with a stun gun," Carmen muttered. There

was both urgency and pain in her voice. "And someone clubbed me on the head. I didn't see the man in time, Duncan. He just charged right at me."

Duncan had to fight the fear that was clawing its way through his throat. "Who charged at you? And where's Joelle?" he couldn't ask fast enough.

"A man wearing a ski mask." Carmen moaned. "There's a hole in the ceiling of your closet, and I think that's how they got in. Through the roof."

Hell. The roof wasn't rigged with the security sensors so an intruder wouldn't have set off the alarms. No one in the house would have known they were about to be attacked.

Duncan hit the accelerator, not heading into the barn but turning around. The tires kicked up clumps of dirt and grass as he sped away.

"God, Duncan," Carmen said. "They took her. They took Joelle."

Chapter Fifteen

Joelle's heart was pounding in her chest. Her breath was gusting. And the fear was right there, clawing away at her.

So much fear for her precious baby.

But she wasn't fighting as the two thugs manhandled her out of the house, down the porch and into the backyard. Not fighting. She had to get away from them, but she couldn't do that now.

Not with one of them holding a stun gun directly against her stomach.

She had no idea what a stun gun would do to the baby, but it couldn't be good. No. She had to wait for a safer way to try to escape, and she had to pray that opportunity would happen soon. Especially since they had gotten her out of Duncan's house and were taking her heavens knew where.

At least they hadn't killed her on sight, and she didn't think they'd killed Carmen or Luca, either. While one of the goons had used her as a human shield—after he'd knocked away her gun—he had held her at bay with the stunner. The other one had used a stun gun on Luca, and Joelle had seen him drop to the floor. Hard. Maybe hard enough to crack his skull.

Carmen had come at the hulking attacker, and she'd had her gun drawn, but she hadn't got off a shot before the thug hit her with a billy club. Carmen went down, too, and then the men had dragged Joelle toward the back of the house.

Now she had to pray they didn't shoot the ranch hands.

Since the hands were at the front of the house, they didn't have the best angle to see what was going on, but if they did, hopefully they'd take cover and call—

She mentally stopped right there.

Someone would call Duncan. If not the hands, eventually Carmen or Luca would do that when they were able. And Duncan would come for her.

Which was possibly what these thugs wanted.

The chance to have her while also forcing Duncan to put his own life in danger to save her and the baby. Was that the thugs' intention? Or would they try to get as far away from Duncan and the other cops as possible? She just didn't know, but she had to be ready for either of those things to happen.

"Was that really my mother who called me?" she asked. Not that she especially wanted to know the answer, not at the moment anyway, but if one of them spoke, she might recognize the voice and then she could know who was doing this.

Not Kate.

She was the only one of their suspects who couldn't be dragging her past Duncan's barn. Of course, Kate could have hired the pair, but it was possible one of the men was either Hamlin or Brad. The smaller goon was the right size to be one of them. But neither of them spoke. They just kept moving.

Joelle tried to tamp down the panic that was threatening to consume her. Hard to do, though, when everything was at risk. Her breathing didn't help. Way too fast. Way too shallow, and it didn't help that the air felt so heavy, like wet wool.

Soon, those heavy clouds would unleash a bad storm, and she figured that wouldn't help matters. It'd mean Duncan would be driving through that to get to her.

The manhandling continued toward the back of the barn, and Joelle heard someone shout. Carmen. The deputy was calling out to the ranch hands for help. That caused both alarm and relief for Joelle. Carmen was alive, but Joelle also didn't want the ranch hands gunned down if they charged at them. Hopefully, the hands would use caution if they figured out where she was.

Once her attackers were behind the barn, they kept moving. Kept dragging her, and just ahead she spotted an old ranch trail. They were commonplace in the area, and this one had a spattering of trees flanking it. A car was there, tucked in between the shadows of those trees. Definitely not visible from the house.

"Where are you taking me?" Joelle asked, trying to make that sound like a demand.

Of course, they didn't answer, which meant they either had orders not to speak to her or there was the real possibility that she would be able to ID one of them from his voice. The men just kept moving until they reached the car, and they shoved her into the back seat.

Since the maneuver caused the stun gun to shift away from her stomach, Joelle tried to pivot so she could do something to escape. But the bulkier man pointed at her with the billy club. The threat was clear. He'd hit her if she tried anything.

She stayed put.

The big guy got in the back seat with her, and the other man jumped behind the wheel. He drove out of there fast. Not heading toward the house, of course, but rather using the trail. She had no idea where it led. They obviously did, though, since they had driven it to get to Duncan's.

She glanced around for anything she could use as a weapon. And she froze. Not because there was something that could help her defend herself but because of the photos.

Dozens of them scattered on the floor of the car.

The pictures of her father. Bleeding. Dying. The same ones that'd been left on the side of the ranch house.

Her gaze fired to the big thug, and while she could see his eyes, there was nothing. No concern that he had just kidnapped a pregnant cop. No worry that she'd just seen photos that could link him to her previous attack.

And to her father's murder.

She hadn't needed any further proof that this was a hired gun. A person capable of cold-blooded murder.

"Did you kill him?" she had to ask.

Still no reaction, though, she heard the driver. He growled out a "shut up." Maybe meant for her. Maybe meant for the big guy as a reminder not to say anything. Either way, the two words had been so low that she hadn't been able to tell if this was Hamlin or Brad who were both out on bail. It was possibly neither of them since the driver could be a hired gun as well. This way, their boss took no risks and kept their hands clean.

Her body shifted and leaned as the driver threaded the car around the ranch trail, and Joelle pushed all thoughts of their suspects aside. Instead, she tried to focus on the shifting and leaning. If she timed it right, she might be able to shove herself against the big guy. Might be able to ram her elbow into his gut and strip him of that billy club and stun gun. But any hopes of that vanished when the driver came off the trail and onto the road.

Joelle glanced around again to get her bearings, and she

recognized where she was. It was, indeed, the road that led to Saddle Ridge, and to the interstate, but they weren't heading in that direction. Just the opposite.

The driver didn't stay on the road for long, though. He took another turn onto another ranch trail. The car bobbled over the uneven surface, and Joelle knew even if she managed to somehow jump from the vehicle, she could be killed since there were thick trees on both sides of this trail.

The minutes crawled by before the car exited out onto another road. She recognized this one as well. And her heart dropped when she realized where they were going.

"You're taking me to my family's ranch," she muttered.

Neither man responded, but Joelle didn't need their confirmation. This wasn't the main route to get to the ranch. This was a much less traveled farm road, one she'd used as a teenager to learn to drive.

They were taking her to Duncan at her family's ranch.

But she immediately rethought that. Duncan would almost certainly be on his way back to his place. And he would be driving the usual faster route. He wouldn't see her. In fact, maybe these goons were taking her there to hand her off to someone. To their boss. Though Joelle couldn't figure out why they'd choose her family ranch for the exchange, she knew she had to be ready to try to escape.

The goon behind the wheel took the turn onto the ranch grounds. Again, not the usual front driveway but rather the back trail that led from the road to the pasture. It was dirt and gravel, not paved like the other, but it was in decent enough shape since it's how her father had often had hay and feed delivered to the barn.

Even though it was hard for her to see the front driveway, Joelle did her best to look around and tried to spot Duncan. Or Woodrow and Ronnie since they were backup.

She couldn't see any of them so it was entirely possible that the two deputies had followed Slater and him back to Duncan's place.

And that could be what the goons had counted on.

Maybe that's why they'd left Luca and Carmen alive. It would have ensured one of them would be able to call for help, and Duncan would come running. Once he arrived at his place, though, Duncan would see she wasn't there.

Would he think to come back here?

It was possible, but it was just as likely he'd be frantically trying to shut down the interstate exits and roads to try and stop the goons from getting her out of the area.

The driver pulled to a stop at the end of the road. Directly in front of the back door of the barn. The loading door was wide enough to accommodate a vehicle, but he didn't open it and park inside where the vehicle would be out of sight. However, he did park, and he immediately got out, throwing open the door on her side and pulling her out. He put the stun gun to her stomach again.

Goon number two made a fast exit, too, and he hurried to his partner so he could hook his arm around Joelle's waist and get her moving. Again, not into the barn but across the backyard.

And that's when Joelle realized where they were taking her.

They were dragging her straight toward the well.

DUNCAN WANTED TO smash his fist into the steering wheel. But that wouldn't help him get to Joelle. Still, the smashing would give him a hard jolt of pain that might rid him of some of the anger, fear and frustration bubbling up inside him. Then again, nothing would help that.

Nothing but finding Joelle and making sure she was safe.

Slater was on the phone to Carmen, and since the call was on speaker, Duncan was hearing what a hellish situation was waiting for him at his place. The ambulance was on the way to get Luca who apparently had a head injury. Carmen had one as well and was bleeding from being hit. And while all of that was important, it wasn't at the top of his worry list.

Joelle was.

And she hadn't been seen since two masked SOBs took her. The ranch hands hadn't spotted anyone. Hadn't seen a vehicle. That could mean the kidnappers had taken Joelle into the barn and were waiting for some kind of showdown. But it was just as likely they'd had a vehicle on one of the ranch trails and used that to escape with her. If so, she could be anywhere by now.

Duncan couldn't let that thought linger in his head. Like bashing his fist on the steering wheel, it wouldn't help, and right now, he just had to focus.

Where would they take her?

And why?

For the baby? So they could wait until she delivered and then try to sell the child? Maybe. But like the other times he'd considered that, it just didn't feel right. Four months was a long time to hold a woman, and if it was the baby they wanted, then why not wait to take her until closer to her due date?

Because this was about revenge.

Of course, that didn't rule out any of their suspects. Hamlin had been riled at Joelle's father for alerting the authorities about the sale of his baby. Hamlin could have decided to aim that anger at Joelle. But Brad hated Sheriff McCullough, too, and he had a beef with everyone in the sheriff's department over Shanda's arrest.

That left Kate.

Joelle's father had been investigating the sale of babies. Had his investigation led him to Kate, and had she silenced the sheriff before he could arrest her? If so, maybe Kate believed that Joelle would follow the same trail as her father and that trail would eventually lead her to Kate.

Of course, none of those theories addressed the baby. And maybe their child didn't directly play into this. It was possible the person doing this didn't want to kill a pregnant woman.

In the background of Slater's phone call, Duncan could hear the wail of sirens approaching his place. He also heard something else, the dinging sound that Slater had an incoming call.

"It's Woodrow," Slater said. "Carmen, I'll call you right back," he added, and he switched to the incoming.

Duncan immediately thought of the heat source they'd seen on infrared in the barn. Possibly Joelle's mother. Or another hostage. And that's why Duncan had had Slater call Woodrow and Ronnie and tell them to stay at the McCullough ranch. Not by the barn, either, in case the person inside turned out to be a gunman. But rather Duncan had wanted them to pull the cruiser out of sight and keep watch of the barn. Hopefully, things hadn't gone to hell in a handbasket there.

"Slater," Woodrow said the moment he was on the line, and Duncan could hear the urgency in the deputy's voice. "A dark blue car just approached the barn from the pasture side of the property."

It took Duncan a second to realize that Woodrow was talking about the McCullough ranch and not Duncan's place. "Is Joelle in the car?" Duncan couldn't ask fast enough.

"I'm pretty sure she is," Woodrow was equally quick to

answer. "There's a woman in the back seat that I believe is Jo-elle. There are two people with her, both wearing ski masks."

Hell. They had taken her there and that made Duncan even more suspicious of that heat source. The killer could be inside the barn.

Duncan slammed on the brakes, and even though the road was narrow, he executed a U-turn to get them headed back to his place. He only hoped he was in time to stop whatever was about to happen.

"We're on our way back there," Slater explained to Wood-row. He glanced at Duncan. "You want Woodrow and Ron-nie to move in or wait for us to get there?"

This might turn out to be a "damned if he did, damned if he didn't" situation, and it could put Woodrow and Ron-nie at extreme risk. Still, Duncan didn't have a lot of op-tions here.

"Woodrow, move in if they get Joelle out of the car," Duncan instructed the deputy. "Do as quiet of an approach as you can manage. I want you to try to sneak up on them and see if you can get her away from them. We'll be there as fast as we can."

Slater ended the call so that Woodrow could get started on that, and then Slater phoned Carmen back to fill her in on what was happening. Or rather what they thought was happening. Duncan wasn't sure what the hell was going on, but if these SOBs hurt Joelle, he was going to rip them to pieces.

Duncan drove too fast and had to fight to keep the cruiser on the road when he took one of the many curves. He had to push. Had to get to Joelle. Because he could be wrong about the boss not wanting to kill a pregnant woman. This could be a sick attempt to use her to replay her father's murder.

Duncan had to stop thinking like that.

"We'll get to her in time," Slater muttered under his breath when he finished his call with Carmen.

Duncan prayed he was right, and he kept up the speed, eating up the distance to the ranch. He was still a good two minutes out when Slater's phone rang again.

"It's Woodrow," Slater said, taking the call on speaker.

"Ronnie and I are out of the cruiser and are approaching the barn on foot," Woodrow said in a whisper. "They just took Joelle out of the car, and one of them has a stun gun pointed at her belly."

That gave Duncan a nasty punch of fear and adrenaline. "Is she injured?" he managed to ask.

"I don't think so." Woodrow paused a heartbeat. "I don't have a clean shot," he added. "They're holding her close."

Duncan got another of those nasty punches. They were using Joelle to protect their sorry butts. "Are they taking her to the house?" Specifically, to the front door so they could recreate the murder.

Woodrow wasn't so quick to answer this time. "No. They're taking her to the well."

Duncan went stiff with surprise. Then, dread. Pure, sick dread.

They were planning to toss her in.

"If we don't get there in time," Duncan said, his voice strangled now from the tight muscles in his throat, "move in to save her. Save her, Woodrow. Don't let her die."

"I won't," Woodrow assured him.

And Woodrow would try. Even if it meant giving up his own life, both Woodrow and Ronnie would attempt to save her. That could get them all killed. But Duncan had to hold on to the hope that all of them would make it out of this alive.

Had to.

Because he couldn't imagine a life without Joelle.

Woodrow ended the call, no doubt so he could focus on getting to Joelle. Duncan focused, too, and he decided not to go with a quiet approach. That would eat up precious time since he would have to park at the end of the driveway and run to the well. Instead, he turned on the sirens, hoping it would distract the two men and cover up any sounds from Woodrow and Ronnie's approach.

Duncan took the turn into the ranch, the cruiser practically flying when he slammed on the accelerator again. Everything inside him was yelling for him to get to Joelle.

He spotted the car in the pasture by the barn. Then, he spotted Joelle. She was, indeed, being used as a shield for two masked men. But she was alive. For now, anyway. She was also right next to the well, and one of the snakes holding her stooped down to shove the cover of the well aside.

Duncan couldn't be sure, but he figured both men were looking at his cruiser now. Joelle certainly was, and he saw the mix of emotions on her face. The fear. The hope. The extreme sense of dread that their baby wasn't safe.

That none of them were.

He fired some glances around, to see if there were any other gunmen lying in wait. No sign of them, but Duncan did spot Woodrow and Ronnie. They were skulking toward the barn, staying on the side where the two thugs hopefully wouldn't be able to see them.

Duncan drove through the yard until one of the thugs motioned for him to stop. That wouldn't have caused him to hit the brakes, but then the thug's partner yanked back Joelle's head, using the choke hold he now had on her. Duncan stopped about thirty feet away, drew his gun and threw open his door. He used the door as a shield and took aim, even though he had nowhere near a clean shot. On the other side of the cruiser, Slater did the same.

Neither man spoke, but the bigger one of the two continued to hold Joelle while the other looped a rope around her. Not in the usual way someone would tie up a person. This was more like a harness that they looped around her bottom.

When the two goons started to move Joelle, Duncan's heart slammed against his chest. They were going to put her in the well. Duncan tried not to look at Joelle's face since he knew that would be too much of a distraction. Instead, he focused on the men, waiting for one of them to move so he could take the shot.

But that didn't happen.

He could only watch as Joelle clutched the rope, and the goons began to lower her into the well.

"Shoot me or my hired help, and we drop her," the smaller man said.

And that's when Duncan knew who was behind this. Because he instantly recognized the voice.

Brad.

JOELLE CURSED WHEN she heard Brad's voice. Everyone in the sheriff's office had searched nonstop to find out the identity of their attacker, and now they had confirmation of who it was with just that handful of words.

Shoot one of us, and we drop her.

And they would. They already had her over the opening of the well, but she had no idea why. If they wanted her dead, why not just kill her…

That thought immediately stopped because she knew why. A moment later Brad confirmed that, too.

"We're going to play a game, Sheriff Holder," he said, his voice dripping with venom. Brad yanked off his ski mask. "You and Slater McCullough are going to die. No way around that," he added in a snarl. "Joelle, too, but you can make her death painless or a nightmare."

It was already a nightmare. She was literally hovering over a well that was at least a hundred feet deep. The sides were narrow so it was possible she could try to hold on, but she wouldn't be able to do that for long. Brad had a grip on the end of the rope, but there were no guarantees whatsoever that he wouldn't just let her drop.

"What the hell do you want?" Duncan snarled.

"Revenge," Brad spat out just as the first drops of rain started to fall. "For ruining my life. For bringing me to this."

"You brought yourself to this," Joelle muttered.

Brad apparently heard her because he made a feral sound of outrage. "You and your fellow cops arrested Shanda. You caused her to miscarry," he shouted.

"And you killed her," Joelle said. Yes, it was a risk to agitate him like this, but the agitation might distract him so that Duncan and Slater could shoot him.

No feral sound this time. Brad made more of a hoarse sob. "That was an accident. She was going to the cops because she thought I'd killed Sheriff McCullough, and I had to stop her." He sounded genuinely sorry about that. And maybe he was.

"You had to stop her," Joelle repeated, and she managed to keep her voice calm. "But you couldn't reason with her."

From the corner of her eye, she saw Woodrow peer around the side of the barn, and she felt another surge of hope. If Duncan and her brother didn't get a shot, then maybe Woodrow could.

"Yes," Brad muttered, and it seemed for a few moments, he was lost in some memories with Shanda. "The hired guns, too, since they chickened out after taking the dispatcher who helped arrest Shanda. Not Arlo, though. He tried and tried hard. So did Willie Jay, and he knew to do the right thing after he was caught."

"I'm guessing Willie Jay knew he was a dead man once he was in custody so he ended things," Duncan said.

"He did the right thing," Brad emphasized. "Not my mother, though. She was going to rat me out, just like Shanda," he added in a mutter that was coated with pain.

"Is your mother alive?" Duncan asked.

"Of course." The pain in his eyes evaporated, and Brad's gaze flicked to the barn. "She's, uh, waiting her turn. I've already planted some records for the withdrawals from the bank to point to that idiot Hamlin hiring some muscle to carry out the kidnappings and such, and now I'll walk away," he said.

Oh, mercy. If Kate was in the barn, Brad probably didn't have plans for her to come out. He would likely kill her and pin that on Hamlin, too.

Then, Joelle had a sickening thought. What if Brad had managed to get his hands on Molly? She could be in the barn right now, gagged, unable to call out for help.

"You waited a long time to come after us," Duncan said, his gaze fixed on Brad. "It's been five months since you murdered Sheriff McCullough."

"I didn't kill him," Brad snapped, and the grip tightened on the rope, yanking Joelle back and nearly causing her to fall in the well. "Shanda thought I did, and I was afraid she'd be able to convince you that I had. Convince you enough to arrest me. But I didn't kill him. Someone beat me to it."

Joelle hadn't thought anything else could add to her grief, but that did it. From the moment Brad had revealed himself, she'd thought they had found her father's killer. Of course, Brad could be lying.

But why would he?

He'd just confessed to killing Shanda and orchestrating a plot to get revenge for her arrest. Why not just own up to her father's murder if he'd done it?

Because he hadn't, that's why.

Now it was Joelle who had to choke back a sob, and later—sweet heaven, there would be a later—she'd deal with that. For now, though, she had to stay alive and make sure Duncan, Slater, Woodrow and Ronnie did, too.

"Do you have Sandra McCullough?" Duncan asked. "Or was it a recording you spliced together?"

Brad's brief smile gave away his answer, but Brad confirmed it anyway. "Easy to fake a recording when she's blabbed on and on during interviews. I had a lot to work with to create a lure."

Part of her was relieved that Brad didn't have her mother. Joelle had to hope that meant she was alive and would be found.

"So, what now?" Duncan demanded.

"Now, you step away from your cruiser," Brad said, his voice eerily calm. He was blinking hard because the rain was getting in his eyes. "Slater, too."

"Step away so you can gun them down," Joelle spelled out. She saw Woodrow again, and he was on his belly inching closer.

"Of course." Again, Brad's voice stayed calm. "This was the best way I knew to draw them out into the open, and I'll deal with Molly later. She's the only one left, and then all the loose ends will be tied up."

"My baby is not a loose end." In contrast, there was plenty of anger in Joelle's voice. "She's an innocent victim in all of this."

"I know. And I'm sorry about that. I am," Brad repeated when she glared at him. "But I'll make this fast. Once Duncan and Slater are dead, then I can finish you fast. You won't feel a thing."

Joelle doubted that, and when Brad started to glance around, she knew she had to do something to pull his attention back to her. "Slater had nothing to do with Shanda's arrest."

Fresh rage flared in Brad's eyes. "He's his father's son, and if he'd been on duty, he would have taken part in it." He shifted those anger-filled eyes to Duncan. "You've got five seconds to step away from the cruiser." And he started the countdown. "One, two, three—"

Before he could get to four, Joelle caught onto the rope and gave it a quick hard jerk. It did what she wanted. It off-balanced Brad. But it did the same to her, and Joelle had to struggle to catch hold of the sides of the well so she wouldn't fall and plunge to the bottom. She scrambled onto the ground, clutching at the grass to make sure she didn't slip back into the gaping hole.

Brad cursed, calling her a vile name, but the sound of the gunshot stopped his profanity tirade. A split second later, there was another blast. Then, a third.

Behind her, the big thug fell. The headshot had made sure of that. Brad, however, stayed on his feet. Frozen with his face pale with shock. He dropped the rope, clutching his left hand to his chest.

Where the blood was spreading fast.

"I'm not sorry," Brad muttered, his gaze fixed on Joelle. "I wish I could have killed you." He pressed something in his pocket before he slumped lifelessly to the ground.

Behind them, fire erupted around the barn.

Chapter Sixteen

Duncan had already started running toward Joelle before he even saw Brad press whatever he'd had in his pocket. Some kind of detonation device no doubt.

The last ditch act of a dying man to kill the person in the barn.

Joelle moved fast, too, hurrying toward the barn. "Molly or Kate could be in there."

Yeah, the heat source they'd seen on infrared could definitely be one of them, but it was equally possible this was another hired gun, lying in wait to finish what his boss had started. That's why Duncan raced ahead of Joelle.

Slater hurried in to help, too. "Joelle, make sure Brad and his hired help aren't anywhere near weapons," Slater told her.

That accomplished two things. Joelle would no longer be close to the barn, and Duncan definitely didn't want Brad or the thug to try any retaliation if they'd managed to survive the gunshots. He was pretty sure they hadn't, but it was too big of a risk to take.

Woodrow hurried to help Joelle, and Ronnie stood guard, making sure no one else was about to launch an attack. Duncan reached the barn first and was thankful that most of the flames were on the sides of the building. Not for long, though. Brad had obviously used some kind of accelerant because the fire was quickly eating its way to the door.

Duncan threw open the barn door and immediately stepped to the side in case he was about to be gunned down. But no shots came his way. Smoke did, though, thick billowing clouds of it. Something that had no doubt been part of Brad's sick plan. The rain would help, some, with the flames, but if the fire didn't kill the person inside, smoke inhalation might.

Even though the storm had blocked out so much of the light, Duncan still spotted the figure on the ground in the center of the barn. "Kate," he muttered. She was trussed up and gagged, but she was conscious and trying to move.

Duncan didn't take the time to untie her. He scooped her up and started toward the door. Not a second too soon. The fire must have triggered some kind of secondary device because the back wall of the barn burst into flames. That got Duncan moving even faster, and in that short distance, the smoke was already clogging his throat and lungs.

The rain was definitely welcome when he darted out into it, and he continued to run, continued to get Kate and himself as far away from the barn as possible. Because there could be another device, one meant to bring the whole barn down, and he didn't want Kate or anyone else hit with fiery debris.

"I just called for an ambulance," Joelle said, hurrying to help him with Kate when Duncan placed the woman on the ground. He got to work on removing the ropes while Joëlle tackled the gag.

"Brad's going to kill all of you and set me up for it," Kate blurted the moment she could speak. "He bragged to me about, egging on that PI so he'd look guilty of these attacks."

"Yes," Duncan confirmed. "Brad admitted to planting some evidence that would point to Hamlin."

"Did he also tell you he drugged me?" Kate asked, and Duncan shook his head, though he'd suspected that's what had happened. "He said he drugged my tea, and then he cursed because I apparently didn't drink enough of it. He wanted me unconscious so he could kill me. But I managed to get out of the house and go to Saddle Ridge."

Duncan nodded since that worked with his theory, too. Brad would have eliminated his mother so she wouldn't tell the cops about him, and then he could have chalked up her death to Hamlin.

"Brad spooked me into leaving the hospital," Kate murmured. "I thought he was going to sneak in and kill me. That's why I ran." She squeezed her eyes shut a moment and shook her head. "At least I tried to run, but one of Brad's hired thugs caught me."

Duncan hated to question the woman, but while they were waiting on that ambulance, she might be able to provide him with more answers. A big one in case any other lives were at stake. "Did Brad say anything about the PI's sister?"

"Isla," Kate was quick to say. "Yes. Brad did more bragging about her, too. He took her a month ago when he started setting all this up. He said she was insurance. That if the cops didn't arrest Hamlin for murder, he would use Isla to force Hamlin to do it. And that if the cops did arrest him, then he could still sell the baby when she had it and then get rid of Isla."

Duncan cursed. "Where was Brad holding Isla?"

Kate shook her head again. "He didn't say. Maybe at his house in San Antonio? It's a big place, and he told me he'd closed off the second floor because he never used it."

Before Duncan could even ask, Slater was taking out his phone. "I'll get SAPD out there right now to do a search."

Good. He prayed she was there and safe. He didn't want Brad to add any more victims to his list.

"My son was a very sick, very disturbed man." Kate's gaze slid to the bodies, and a hoarse sob tore from her throat.

"One of them is Brad," Duncan told her. Not the best way to do a death notification, but she had to know. "I stopped him."

Kate looked up at him, and a mix of both tears and rain slid down her cheeks. "You did what you had to do," she muttered.

He had, and while Duncan didn't need Kate's validation about that, he was glad she didn't appear to be on the verge of being hysterical with grief. But there would be grief. He was sure of that, and somehow Kate would have to try to come to terms with what her son had done.

And what Brad had done was create a nightmare.

Five dead hired guns. Duncan wouldn't mourn that. But he was desperately sorry for the hellish memories Brad had given Joelle, Molly and Kate. Hell, had given him, too, because he doubted he'd ever be able to forget the terror of Brad coming so close to putting Joelle in that well.

One thing that Duncan was certain of was that Kate had had no part in her son's plan. That was good for tying up the loose ends of the investigation, but again, Kate would have to deal with her son pulling her into all of this.

Duncan looked at Joelle, their gazes connecting, and he didn't care who was watching. He pulled her into his arms and kissed her. There was both relief and hope in that kiss. Relief that she and their baby were alive. Hope that nothing like this would ever happen to them again.

"SAPD already had officers in the area of Brad's house, and they're going in right now," Duncan heard Slater say, and he looked up to see Joelle's brother watching them. Well, watching as much as the rain would allow. It was coming down hard now.

Woodrow was heading to the back of the ranch house, and Ronnie was near the bodies. The chaos of a crime scene had already gotten started.

"Woodrow's getting some umbrellas from the house," Slater explained. "We won't move Kate any more than necessary until the EMTs give us the okay, but why don't Joelle and you go wait on the porch? No need for all of us to get soaked."

Duncan didn't care about the "getting soaked" part, but he wanted Joelle off her feet. Of course, she'd need another exam at the hospital, but he wanted to check for himself to make sure she hadn't physically been harmed.

Even though he figured it wasn't necessary, Duncan scooped her up in his arms and carried her to the porch. She didn't balk. In fact, she sighed and buried her face against his neck. He held her that way for several moments until they were beneath the porch roof. Then, he eased her back to her feet so he could kiss her.

It was another of those comfort kisses, and she didn't balk about that, either. Just the opposite. She returned the kiss, making it long, hard and deep.

"I thought Brad was going to shoot you," she said when she finally pulled back. She looked at him, examining him as he was doing to her.

Duncan didn't voice his fears about what he thought Brad would do to her. No need. They both knew how close they'd all come to dying.

"I think Brad was telling the truth when he said he didn't kill my father," Joelle muttered.

He nodded. And wished it weren't true. Because if Brad had killed Sheriff McCullough, then that would have given them all some closure. It would have closed the case, and they could have started the process of moving on. From that, anyway. In other ways, Duncan felt as if Joelle and he had, indeed, moved on.

In the best possible direction.

He hoped he wasn't wrong.

"I'm in love with you, Joelle," he said, "and I'm sorry I didn't tell you that sooner. I'm sorry that it took us almost dying for me to realize that I love you and I want a life with you and our baby."

Duncan braced for her reaction, which he knew could be a shake of her head and a reminder that the timing was all wrong for this. That the timing might never be right.

But that didn't happen.

Joelle smiled. Actually, smiled. And like the kiss, Duncan felt as if it lifted a whole mountain of weight off his shoulders. He would have kissed her again to taste that smile, but Slater called out to them.

"The cops found Isla," Slater said, adding a fist pump of celebration. "She's alive and as well as she can be. They're transporting her to the hospital as soon as the ambulance arrives."

"Did she have the baby?" Joelle asked.

Slater shook his head. "She's due in a couple of weeks." He motioned toward his phone. "Should I call Hamlin and let him know?"

"Call him," Duncan verified. From everything that Kate and Brad had said, Hamlin hadn't been responsible for any of this mess.

Slater moved away to do that, and Duncan turned back to Joelle to give her that kiss. But she beat him to it and kissed him first. She seemed to pour everything into it. Especially her heart. It turned way too hot, considering they were on a porch with a yard full of cops and the approaching sirens from an ambulance and more cruisers.

Joelle didn't break the kiss until there was a risk of passing out from lack of oxygen, and when she finally did pull back, she laughed.

"I'm in love with you, too, Duncan," she said, pinning her gaze to his. They were eye to eye. Mouth to mouth. Breath to breath. "And, no, that's not the adrenaline crash talking. Or the effects of that kiss. Though it was pretty potent," she added in a mutter.

Now he laughed, and he let the heat and the joy of the moment wash over him. Duncan knew it would be the start of more moments just like this one. With the woman he loved and their baby.

* * * * *

Don't miss
Protecting the Newborn,
the second book in USA TODAY *bestselling author
Delores Fossen's miniseries, Saddle Ridge Justice,
available next month!*